BEWITCHING ANDIE

Baga Shores Romance Book One

Candace Colt

Copyright © 2022 by Candace Colt, Author

All rights reserved. No part of this book may be reproduced in any form or by any electronic or mechanical means, including information storage and retrieval systems—except in the case of brief quotations embodied in critical articles or reviews—without permission in writing from the author.

This book is a work of fiction. All characters, events, scenes, plots, and associated elements remain the exclusive copyrighted and trademarked property of Candace Colt, Author. Any similarity to actual persons, living or dead, is purely coincidental and not intended by the author.

Published in the United States of America

Paperback ISBN 979-8-9857061-0-9

eBook ISBN 979-8-9857061-1-6

Cover Design: Susan Smith sesmithfl.com

Learn more about the author CandaceColt.com

BEWITCHING ANDIE

The problem with magic is that it doesn't always work the way you want....

Andie McCraig is not only a single mom—she's also a witch! Unfortunately, she isn't a very good one. When her young son courts danger by flaunting his emerging Draiocht gift, she has no other choice but to return home to Baga Shores.

The last thing Brett Austin wants is a protégé. He renounced his gift long ago and has no intentions of being a mentor, much less a role model, to a powerful young Draiocht with a mother who couldn't cast a proper spell if her life depended on it!

A frightening prediction changes Brett's mind. As danger swirls around the enchanting small town of Baga Shores, Brett soon realizes he and Andie must work together to protect her son.

Can Brett let go of the past long enough to help Andie, or will he fail again—this time losing everything important to him?

CANDACE COLT

BEWITCHING ANDIE is the first book in the Baga Shores Romance Series and is perfect for fans of feel-good, sweet romance, lovable magical characters, and enchanting small towns.

Chapter One

Stop and go. Stop and go. Stop and *stop*.

Noon hour traffic on the W. A. Goodfellow Causeway across Tampa Bay was horrifying. Something Andie McCraig had forgotten, and for two good reasons.

First, it was a pain to keep shifting gears in her MINI Cooper. Second, they'd come to a dead halt at the top of the bridge. Andie hated bridges, even relatively low ones like the Goodfellow.

She squeezed one hand around the gearshift handle and the other on the steering wheel as she waited for that blessed moment they'd start moving again. It didn't look promising from the obnoxious red stripe indicator on her car's navigation screen. And it didn't help her attitude that oncoming traffic sailed past.

Her seven-year-old son, Sam, had been patient for the six-hour drive from the Florida panhandle across I-10 and the crawl through bumper-to-bumper traffic on south I-75. But she could tell he was getting antsy. The truth was, so was she. Relaxing was a top priority once they got to her grandmother's house.

"This will break up any minute." She hoped that was true for Sam's sake. It had been a long time since the last rest stop.

Andie craned her neck to see around the SUV, but nothing moved ahead. There must have been a wreck. She glanced in her rearview mirror to get an idea of how many were lined up behind. And to watch that guy still sitting on a motorcycle behind her. If he'd revved that engine once, he'd done it ten times. Did he think that would make this line move faster?

Her stomach rumbled again in a not-so-gentle reminder that she hadn't eaten anything since McDonald's three hours ago. Sam tapped her arm and held up an open bag of chocolate chip cookies.

That he could hear that muffled growl was another reminder of the child's gift of sharp senses.

"Thanks, honey." She popped one of the last broken pieces in her mouth.

By some miracle, cars in front of them began creeping forward. Andie put the Cooper in gear and edged along with them. Once they were back up to speed, and there was a space in the next lane over, the motorcycle man gunned it and dashed around her. She watched him change lanes again before he disappeared up ahead.

While parked on the bridge, catching glimpses of him in the mirror had been an enjoyable distraction. She had imagined him to be tattooed from toes to nose. He probably had a bevy of girlfriends, but she noticed the Harley didn't have a passenger seat when he passed her.

She had given entirely too much time to this daydream. It was time to refocus on Sam and how this meeting with his great-grandmother would go. It better go *well* since this was Andie's only hope for help.

Finally, the "Welcome to Baga Shores" sign was in sight. The last four blocks were a breeze. The house was just up ahead and not a minute too soon.

Andie McCraig swerved into the driveway and slammed on the breaks.

Impossible. *That* Harley and *that* rider?

The man swung a long, muscular leg over the seat and dismounted. Standing with his back to her car, the man removed his helmet and scuffed his fingers through his brown hair.

The man turned, and his annoying scowl softened as he slipped off his sunglasses.

She got out of the car and leaned against the door as the man walked toward her. The corners of his eyelids crinkled as his face brightened into a smile.

"Hey, Andie," he said in a deep, heart-grabbing voice. "That was you in front of me?"

The neatly cropped beard and mustache caught her off guard. So did his body-hugging T-shirt, which outlined the impressive arms and broad chest she'd shamelessly ogled earlier in the rearview mirror. She stared a few more moments.

"You don't recognize me, do you?" he asked.

Holy mother-of-pearl! Brett Austin? The skinny dweeb who'd hung around here with her brother, Jason? Of all places in the world, why had he parked a motorcycle in her grandmother's driveway?

Sam had gotten out and stood in front of the four-car garage in a split second. Before she could gasp a breath or utter a polite greeting to Brett, Sam had raised a finger, and without touching anything, he opened one door halfway. Andie tipped her head to the heavens.

As if raising this boy by herself wasn't hard enough.

After an exhausting all-day drive, she didn't want to say anything to set him off. Besides, he'd been a little trooper. Before dawn, they'd left the only home he'd ever known. She doubted he understood they would never go back there, either.

What choice did she have? Her ex-husband's monthly support payments barely covered expenses. Every job lead dried up as soon as people associated her name with the powerful McCraig family.

Coupled with stories about Sam, spun so out of control it seemed they were about some other kid, it didn't help that he kept lifting things.

"Honey," she said in a measured tone. "Please put the door back down."

Sam paused, his finger frozen in the air, and flashed Andie a mischievous grin.

She knew that look too well. "Slowly, Sam. Do not slam—"

He dropped his hand to his side. The crash of heavy wood hitting concrete chopped her words at the knees. Andie's heart double thumped.

So much for that.

"Very interesting," Brett said.

If anyone, Brett should know about *interesting*. He and half the people in Baga Shores had magical gifts. Sam's demonstration paled compared to what Brett had done as a kid.

"That's my boy." Andie gathered her ankle-length denim skirt, bent to Sam's eye level, and geared up her stern mom voice.

"Honey, what did we talk about? You cannot move things with your fingers." Especially where every eye in town could be on them.

Sam's gaze met hers before it flicked away toward a gecko in the bushes.

She softened her voice. "Honey, I want you to meet Uncle Jason's friend Brett."

Brett squatted beside them and held his hand up for a high five. Sam stared at the man's palm, three times larger than his. He gave Brett a quick hand slap and wiggled away, searching for the lizard.

Brett held Andie's elbow as they stood. "Long day?" he asked.

Longer than he could imagine. "Yeah. But we made it."

"Can I help unload?" Brett asked.

"Uh. No thanks." She turned away quickly to beckon her son to her side. Odd that Brett knew she'd driven a long way today. Who'd told him?

Once Sam was beside her, she offered him her pinky finger. "You know the drill." He hooked his finger into hers.

She caught Brett's confused frown from the corner of her eye, but she continued.

"With mine in yours and yours in mine, we seal a promise by fingers twined." Andie locked her gaze on Sam's. "Now, please don't lift things."

Since Sam's magic had emerged, they'd repeated this promise a hundred times when he opened doors. Or tossed trash bins. Or lifted the school principal's office chair with the principal still sitting in it.

Pinky promises were two-way deals. Keeping her end of each bargain was easy. Since the divorce almost a year ago, her pitiful attempts to revive her gift had been laughable failures. Andie's grandmother, Miriam Pennywick Tanner, or Mimi, descended from a long line of witches. Fat chance she'd support any bargain not to use the craft.

To Andie, there were enough witches in the family to carry on the tradition, and did they ever carry on.

Sam squeezed Andie's hand as the trio walked up five marble steps to the massive wood and glass door of the three story house known to everyone as the sandcastle gone wild. Family lore was that Andie's grandfather had built this house to look like St Pete Beach's Don Cesar-lite. For all intents, he'd succeeded.

Andie let Sam push the doorbell. She'd lived here most of her childhood. Why did she feel like a stranger who had to request entrance?

"Sam, remember our promise," Andie said.

Brett sniffed a laugh. "My mom's warnings never worked on me."

She started to say something but decided against it. Though mute, Sam made up for it with keen hearing. Instead, she flashed Brett a "don't go there" grimace.

Inside, a vacuum motor shut off, and a woman approached, her features distorted through the door's beveled windows. Was this another of Mimi's Ordinary human housekeepers? None of them ever stayed long. Who could blame them? Her grandmother's habit of inviting anyone and anything to visit could be an annoying interruption to household chores.

Two visitors flashed through Andie's mind immediately. One, an eighteenth-century colonial time traveler who'd been gobsmacked by television, soon caught on and lasted an extra two weeks so he could binge-watch *Outlander*.

Andie hadn't been much older than Sam when a shifted male coyote appeared on the deck. Hungry, smelly, and stark naked. She shuddered at the memory.

The front door opened, and a pleasant auburn-haired woman greeted them. She flashed a sky-wide smile.

"Hello, Brett. And you two must be Andarta and Sam. I'm Grace Henderson, Ms. Miriam's housekeeper."

More like the latest housekeeper. She caught Sam's confusion. "Honey, Andarta is my long name. Like yours is Samuel."

Sam hopped from one foot to the other.

"Excuse us a moment." Andie ushered Sam past Grace and into the guest bathroom. She stood outside the closed door as Sam used the toilet. She claimed victory when she heard the reassuring sound that he'd remembered to flush.

He started out the door. "Hands, please." Andie escorted him back to the sink. While he washed, she fiddled with strands of her hair and dug into her purse for lipstick.

"You're lovely, my dear."

Sam snapped to attention and spun toward the woman who stood in the hallway.

Trim and youthful, Mimi hadn't aged a minute. Her eyes were still clear and sharp blue, and her skin smooth as that of women half her age, though her age was anyone's guess. She projected a *Vogue* supermodel image. Her soft silver hair hovered over her shoulders, and her classy white blouse was tucked into navy slacks.

Mimi's embrace was the reassurance that bringing her little boy here was the right decision.

Mimi released Andie and stepped back. A broad smile crossed her face. "Well, Sam, aren't you the fine one? My, how you've grown." Tears briefly brimmed her eyelids. "Come here, young man. The bathroom's not a place for a formal greeting."

Andie put a hand on Sam's back and softly urged him forward. He took a few hesitant steps into the hallway, then stopped.

"You remember Mimi?" she asked.

Sam's baffled frown confirmed that he didn't. How could he? His father had forbidden trips to Baga Shores. All Sam had ever seen were photos of his great-grandmother.

"My goodness, you are handsome." Mimi leaned down and hugged the boy. With one arm around Andie's waist, she held Sam's hand and led them through the house. Surprisingly, Sam kept his grip, too petrified to let go.

"You must try Grace's gumbo," Mimi said.

In the kitchen, Andie watched Brett open one cabinet after another. "All these hinges need is some wood caulk in the screw holes," he said. "No biggie. I can grab some from the restaurant and come back later."

Brett Austin, the little kid who used to pull Andie's pigtails and hadn't seen since she left Baga Shores nearly ten years ago, maneuvered around this kitchen like he owned the place. When Andie and her brother, Jason, grew up in Mimi's house, Brett hung out a lot. Had he become a regular around here?

Brett owned a restaurant from what she gleaned from small talk during lunch. Quite a settled-down kind of thing for Baga's party-boy poster child. His relationship status was a question mark. No news flash there.

"Sorry to break up the party, but I have to leave." Brett took his dishes to the sink. "Andie, I'll be back later. How about I take you and Sam on a boat ride to check out what's changed?"

Boat ride? Andie chewed her bottom lip and glanced between her cherubic-faced son and Brett. Sam swam like a tadpole in a pool, but what if he fell into the Gulf of Mexico? For all she knew, maybe Brett had just been released from prison. Or was on the lam from drug dealers. Or would he bring some sex-starved floozy with him?

It was important for Sam to try new things, but it had been a very long day, and his routine had been screwed up enough. And Andie certainly wasn't ready to be semi-alone with Brett.

"Thanks. Maybe another time," she said.

"No worries." Brett turned his gaze to Sam. "Good to meet you, buddy."

Sam, usually wary of strangers, flashed Brett a quick smile to Andie's surprise.

"Oh, wait," she called after Brett. As she hopped off her stool, her boot heel caught in her hem, resulting in an embarrassingly loud *riiiipppp*. Once again, finesse had eluded her.

"I need to move my car," she said as she untangled her shoe.

"I can get around it." Brett waved over his shoulder as he left.

Grace stopped beside Andie on her way to return the vacuum to the storage closet. "If it makes any difference, I trust Brett completely."

"Absolutely." Mimi paused. "Of course, your decision, dear."

It certainly was her decision.

"It was a nice offer, Mimi, but not the right one for us. Anyway, we should unload the car." She tucked in her torn hem before going to the door.

Sam raced ahead and then stopped short.

His mischievous smile should have alerted Andie. She hesitated a split second too long.

He turned back and wiggled a finger toward the door. When the latch clicked, Andie forgot her rule not to yell at him.

"SAM!"

He dropped his hand to his side.

"Well, what have we here?" Mimi stood with her hands folded behind her back.

While Sam fiddled with objects on a nearby bookshelf, Andie exchanged glances with her grandmother and Grace.

"Speak your mind, child. Grace is a friend," Mimi said.

In Baga Shores, a *friend* meant they were Ordinary humans who understood magicals.

"When I said I wanted to come back home, I left a few things out." She hesitated and searched for the right words. "It seems Sam's a bit of a wizard."

Andie spoke softly so Sam wouldn't overhear. He understood a lot more than people gave him credit for.

"His thing right now is doors. Last month he obsessed over lifting things." Andie didn't have a clue what he'd try next.

Mimi's smile brightened the room. "I knew it! I just knew there was another reason you came home." She raised her hands in joy. "Praise the souls of our ancestors! We must plan a celebration."

Andie pressed her hand to her forehead. She came here to help Sam forget the magic, not celebrate it. "Please, Mimi. Don't encourage him."

"But my dear, our Sam inherited the ancient Draiocht gift! This is a significant milestone."

Right. A *significant milestone* for a nonverbal magical Draio.

Sam halted as they stepped out on the porch, and Andie slammed into him.

"What's wrong?" she asked.

Sam sat down on the stairs and ran his hand over ... nothing.

"Ah, he discovered Alika." Mimi had followed them outside. "Andarta, there's something I should have told you, too."

Relief washed over her as a beautiful black cat came into focus. "You have a new familiar?"

That would be the good news. The bad? Sam saw it before it materialized. Andie would need a lot of help with this boy.

"Alika is not mine," Mimi said.

"I don't understand." Andie darted her gaze to either side. "Whose is it, then?"

A shimmering cloud of pink and purple descended and swirled into a tight funnel. It burst into bright fireworks that rained overhead as Sam gleefully tried to capture the sparkles in his open hands.

The psychedelic display dissipated, revealing a woman with ginger dreadlocks wound into a topknot. She was dressed in an embroidered teal blouse over bohemian harem pants. Her bare feet were adorned in tinkling ankle bracelets.

Open-armed, the woman approached Andie.

Despite the warm June afternoon, a cold chill skimmed over Andie, and she tightened her fists behind her back.

"This is what you failed to tell me?" Andie whispered to Mimi.

"Guess we're even." Mimi gently pressed Andie forward.

"Darling Andarta, how long has it been?" The woman hugged Andie.

Andie returned a lukewarm one. "A very long time." *Mother.*

Chapter Two

"I can't deal with this." Brett shut his laptop and scratched behind the ear of the snoring golden retriever at his feet.

The more he tried to concentrate on numbers, the more frustrated he became. This damn report was due but was a long way from finished. He descended the outdoor steps from his apartment and took a seat at the Dockside Grille's bar. He waved to Robbi Britton, the bartender.

After she wiped the counter in front of him, Robbi served him a glass of iced tea. He proceeded to add five sugar packets.

Robbi chuckled. "Partied a bit too hard, did we?"

"How's that?"

"Oh, I dunno. Your eyes tell me you're wiped out. And you just doctored sweet tea."

"Crap." He pushed the glass away. "Coffee. Black."

Robbi switched the tea for a mug of coffee. "Sorry I couldn't make the celebration last night." Yesterday marked the fifth anniversary of Brett's ownership of the Dockside Grille.

"Apparently, I partied enough for both of us."

Staying in one spot was no small feat. For most of his adult life, Brett had bounced around the world and accomplished not much of anything.

Robbi leaned her five-foot-three body in closer. "So give us the deets on the granddaughter."

Sabrina, the Dockside's assistant manager, slipped beside Brett. "We're all ears."

He stared into his cup. Not only were these women all ears—two pairs of female eyes, Robbi's brown and Sabrina's coal-black, bored through him.

They were ready to pounce on his every nuance like hungry lionesses circling a gazelle. How did the news about Mimi Tanner's houseguest spread so fast? Like he didn't know. This was Baga Shores, a beautiful coastal town situated on a peninsula with water on both sides.

A chamber of commerce dream town so small that poking into each other's business was a favored pastime. And full of freaking nosy Ordinary humans and magicals like Robbi and Sabrina.

Brett cautiously chose his words, grateful that neither woman's gift was mind-reading. Besides, he wasn't sure how to process Jason's sister growing up and with a kid.

He sipped his coffee casually. "She's all right, I guess."

All right? The dark-haired bombshell was gorgeous in that denim skirt and the sexy blouse that hinted at curves.

"So the poor thing's a homely frump, huh?" Sabrina laughed.

He gripped the cup tighter. "I wouldn't say that."

"Ah-ha. Gorgeous, isn't she?" Robbi acknowledged another customer at the end of the bar. "Just when this was getting good. Neither of you says another word till I get back." She tossed the towel over her shoulder and left them.

"I need your help with the books, Sabrina. Nothing makes sense," Brett said.

Sabrina clucked her tongue. "I told you to wait until I had time."

BEWITCHING ANDIE

Brett's brain scrambled numbers, figures, calculations, and spreadsheets. Skilled in business operations that didn't include accounting, he'd hired whip-smart Sabrina.

While they waited for Robbi, Sabrina nervously toyed with the mala beads around her wrist. After a few seconds, she glanced at Brett, but her eyes focused somewhere beyond.

"Something's up. I recognize that look," Brett said.

"Can't tell you what yet." Sabrina, a Draio like him, was also prescient. She moved her head as though tracking something outside her sight. "Does the granddaughter have a child? A boy?"

"Let's give the granddaughter a name, Sabrina. How about we call her Andie? Yes, she has a boy."

"It's something bad. Be careful of somebody who calls him *Sport*." Without another word, Sabrina left the bar and went through the swinging doors to the kitchen.

"That's all you got?" he muttered to himself as he unconsciously rubbed his chest to relieve tightness. He never doubted Sabrina's visions, but she hadn't given him much to go on.

Robbi returned and reached for Brett's empty cup, but he didn't release his death grip. "What did I miss? Where's Sabrina? You look like you've seen a ghost."

"I'm fine," he lied. Even if it was wrong, Sabrina's warning shook him to the marrow. Sam was a cute little kid but seemed like a handful. But what help would he be?

As he started to get up, Robbi stopped him. "Brett, the cup?"

He sniffed a laugh as he handed it to her, then spun around on the barstool. Before going upstairs to his apartment, he paused to look at the framed award over the hostess station. The Dockside Grille was this year's best eatery in Baga Shores.

With a heart full of pride, he looked around the restaurant. Once a crummy dive, the Dockside had transformed into a family friendly Intercoastal waterside eatery. The transformation hadn't been overnight and had taken a lot of work. The old rickety furniture had been replaced. Corny dust-collecting plastic fish and shells on the walls were gone. Fresh paint, new flooring, and lighting brightened the atmosphere.

He'd given the place a second chance, just as his father did for him when he gave him the restaurant.

Time to catch some baseball on TV and not think about Sabrina's vision.

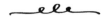

Andie double-checked the deadbolt on the bedroom's balcony door. Logically, it made perfect sense to secure them inside. On the other hand, Sam could open it with a finger flick.

"Honey, come see the gorgeous view of the water from up here."

She'd spent so many hours on that beach with Jason, and loads of cousins building sandcastles, shelling, crabbing, and boogie-boarding.

And fantasizing about a fairy-tale life that never came to be for her.

Sam, who'd remained in the hallway, hesitantly stepped inside, hugging his backpack for dear life. She watched as he scanned the four walls. He loved colorful things, but the explosion of the puked-cotton-candy island motif here had to overwhelm him.

It was nothing like her childhood bedroom. Gone were the *NSYNC posters thumbtacked to every available space. Her bookcase was gone. Her desk was gone.

All were gone except for one familiar item sitting on one of the twin beds.

Propped up between two mango-colored throw pillows was her old American Girl doll. Andie held it for better inspection.

Its brown doe eyes stared back at her. Its freshly laundered outfit smelled of lavender.

"I'm back, Lindsey," Andie whispered as she hugged the doll and carefully put it down.

While she unpacked the clothing items they'd brought with them, Sam sat on the edge of the twin bed next to hers, kicking his heels against the mattress. Andie sensed he was on the verge of another meltdown. She needed to find a quick diversion.

"How about let's go down to the beach?" she offered.

She helped Sam change into his trunks and then went into the bathroom to change into her suit and cover-up. As she adjusted her straw cowgirl hat, she heard Sam's distinctive angry groan.

She flung the door open to find Sam standing amid his color markers strewn everywhere. Andie's mother, Rhea, was on her knees, and her arm stretched under one of the twin beds.

Andie didn't bother to ask what happened. Sam's meltdown was overdue. She really couldn't blame him. His inability to talk often led to restless frustration. She could identify with that. Though she could speak, there'd been many times Andie wanted to throw what she owned to the four winds.

Andie and her mother collected the markers and put them back in the box Sam carried in the backpack.

"He'll be fine, Andarta. It takes time to settle in," Rhea said.

Andie tried to reply, but her throat constricted. How would her mother understand settling anywhere?

Before she was barely out of her teens, Rhea already had two babies: Jason first, followed by Andie, born eighteen months later. Both were healthy and normal by God's grace, except for being born into a witches' lineage.

The only stable home Andie ever had was Mimi's house. Rhea had stayed with them until wanderlust, some spiritual guru, or a new boyfriend seduced her. When each episode failed, and they always did, she drifted back. No explanations. No apologies.

Andie had vague memories of her father, who'd skipped out when she was two. Likewise, what memories would Sam have of his Mister Macho father, an Ordinary who couldn't handle having a son like Sam and had skipped out on them?

"There now," Rhea said. "Let's leave your backpack and drawing things up here and head to the beach."

When Rhea placed them on his bed, Andie braced for another disaster. But Sam seemed okay with Rhea's suggestion.

"Coming with us?" Rhea asked.

"In a minute." Andie pretended to straighten up the already tidy room as she wiped a tear. She popped open the box and organized his color markers.

Andie stepped back when Sam reached for Rhea's outstretched hand, and they started down the stairs. He didn't know Rhea Tanner from a doorknob, yet he went with her anyway. That alone was a bit of magic.

Not ready to call this episode with Rhea a mother-daughter bonding, Andie would take this one thing at a time. But her mother's calm influence on Sam was nothing short of amazing.

She caught up with them as they exited the house through the deck sliders. Outside, they followed a narrow, wooden walkway through a canopy of sea-grape branches. Before stepping onto the sand, they admired the expansive panorama of azure-blue water, something Andie had missed terribly.

Simultaneously, Andie and Rhea took one of Sam's hands, and together, they ran to the water's edge. The frothy tide brought in waves of tiny coquinas, each clam desperately burrowing around their feet as they clamored for survival.

"Try to dig them out. Like this." Rhea wiggled her toes in the wet sand.

Sam giggled as he copied Rhea.

Andie stood back and relished this moment in the warm sun. This was how little boys should play. Wild and free with not a care in the world. Perhaps so should their mothers.

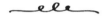

Flipping through TV channels in his quiet bachelor pad wasn't the distraction Brett had hoped for. His mind churned with questions.

Mimi Tanner was the most independent female he knew. Between her and Grace, they could diagnose and fix anything. Why did she ask him to come by to look at cabinet hinges?

He knew Andie was due home, but not at the same time as he was expected. Mimi certainly did.

This smacked of a setup. If that was Mimi's plan, Brett needed to stop her in her tracks.

He grabbed a couple of tools and a tube of wood putty from his supply cabinet, and with Rex at his side, he walked the quarter-mile from his apartment rather than ride the Harley. It would give him more time to think.

Once he approached Mimi's front door, he wondered if he should have brought Rex along. What if Sam was afraid of dogs?

Mimi answered the doorbell. "Oh, good. You're back." Mimi took Brett's tools and set them on the kitchen counter. "The cabinets can wait. Let's go out on the deck."

"Mimi, what are you up to?"

"Not a thing. But I need to talk to you."

She ushered Brett outside with Rex in tow, still holding the old tennis ball he'd carried in his mouth since they left the apartment. Brett had a clear view of Andie and her boy from the deck.

"Mimi, who's that other woman with them?"

"Andie's mother."

"You're kidding." Brett had spent as much time here as he had in his own home as a kid. He'd met Andie's mother maybe once.

"I'm so happy to have them all here," Mimi said.

"I'm sure you are."

Brett wondered if Andie had the same feeling. From what he remembered, Andie, Jason, and their mother didn't have a great relationship.

While he watched, a sudden wind gust lifted Andie's cover-up and revealed her bright blue swimsuit, which hugged her shapely curves. That woman could neutralize a monk's vow, and Brett was no celibate. *Damn. Switch gears.* This was Jason's kid sister.

"How's she doing? I mean with Sam," he said.

"She's still the sweetheart I remember, but the fun has gone out of her. She loves that little boy." After a momentary pause, she added: "And apparently, he has the gift."

The hair raised on the back of his neck. It was starting to make sense. Mimi's request to have him here was more than Brett's "friendly face."

"I suspected when Andarta asked to come home that she had something she was reluctant to tell me. She held back the best part. Imagine how excited I was when he saw my daughter's cat before it materialized. Can you believe it?"

Believe? He saw the kid in action first-hand.

"It concerns me that my granddaughter refused a rite-of-passage celebration for Sam. This is one of the most important events in a young Draio's life." Mimi hooked her arm into Brett's. "Help me change her mind."

"Why me?" He didn't know about those celebrations. They weren't a big deal to his parents. He tried to loosen his arm, but Mimi held firm.

"The boy needs a male role model. You're both Draios. A perfect match."

Oh, sure. A failed Draio would be a perfect match for absolutely nobody. "Mimi, I'm not right for this."

"But you are." Mimi's tone had a solemn ring.

Rex dropped the ragged tennis ball out of his mouth and snapped a loud bark. Brett picked up the ball, bounced it on the wooden deck twice, then drew his arm back and pitched the ball like a missile over the sea grape canopy.

It landed at least three hundred yards beyond the deck.

Mimi tossed her head back and gave a hearty, deep laugh. "See what I mean? You're perfect for this. You still have the power."

"I suppose some of it's still there." But when he needed it, the Draio had failed. Before Brett could stop him, Rex raced full tilt past the ball and straight toward the two women and the boy.

"Stand down!" Brett commanded as he jogged after him.

Rex halted in place as Brett caught up with them.

"Are you okay with my dog being here?" he asked Andie. "I can send him back to the house."

Andie shook her head. "Please don't. Sam loves animals."

Brett gave Rex the release command, and Rex and Sam trotted off like old friends, with Andie's mother skipping along with them.

Andie stepped closer and put her hand on his forearm. "Did my grandmother explain why we're here?"

Was it the warm breeze or her soft touch that sent an electrical charge through him? It would be so easy to take her into his arms. *Crazy! Get a grip!* He wished she would move her hand away. Soon.

Before he could answer, Rex and a laughing Sam raced around them. The dog and the boy circled and changed directions. When Sam's feet caught on the third pass, he fell against his mother.

Knocked off-balance, Andie tumbled to her knees. Her fingers tightened around Brett's arm.

Her sunglasses tipped at an angle, allowing him a glimpse of her sparkling dark brown eyes. For an instant, her parted lips hinted at something more than surprise. She scrambled to stand up, straightened the sunglasses, and her sexy look vanished in the wind.

Think about something else. Anything. Right. Tell that to the lower forty-eight.

They stood discreetly apart as she dusted the sand from her legs. While Sam and Rex continued their game of chase, Brett rifled his brain to say something clever.

"Rex gets a little rambunctious sometimes," he said.

"I'm just happy Sam's playing with the dog. It's hard for him to make human friends when he can't communicate with spoken words."

"Jason told me," Brett said.

Her shoulders relaxed. "I'm glad he did. I don't hide it, but explaining it gets old. Sam's inability to talk has nothing to do with the Draiocht. I worry about what will happen to him as he gets older. It's like a double curse."

Poor kid. Being a Draio was curse enough.

"You know Steven and I are divorced, right?" she asked.

"Jason told me that, too." He didn't know anything about her ex-husband other than Jason thought he was a sleaze. Mimi didn't think highly of the man, either.

"I should get Sam back inside. I don't want him burning to a crisp." She patted her head. "Where'd my hat go?"

"Behind you." Brett took the hat from Rex's mouth and handed it to Andie. She pulled it down to the top of her sunglasses.

Why hide that gorgeous face?

Andie's mother and Sam came up beside her. "Brett, you remember me? I'm Rhea."

Brett shook her hand. "I think I met you once." But he couldn't place when that was.

"You were a little guy about Sam's age when I saw you the last time. How you've grown," Rhea said.

"Rhea, it's time to take Sam in," Andie said.

Thank goodness Andie changed that topic. Small talk with strangers in the Dockside was easy for Brett. But he didn't remember this woman well enough to make conversation.

"Andarta, stay out here. I'm sure you two want to catch up," Rhea said. "Sam and I will be on the deck. Brett, may we take Rex?"

"Fine with me," Brett said.

"We won't go too far," Andie said.

Brett cast his glance over the Gulf. Not going too far sounded like a solid plan.

Chapter Three

Except for a flock of squawking gulls, the beach was deserted. Andie walked backward beside Brett to keep an eye on Sam. A few yards farther, she wouldn't be able to see him.

She found a smooth patch. "Let's stop here."

Andie sat next to Brett and kept an eye on the deck until she was satisfied Sam was okay. Then she followed Brett's gaze toward Lemon Key, a barrier island on the horizon. She, Jason, and her cousins would kayak out there on calm water days. Andie's childhood concept of time centered around school, play, and the next meal. Did Sam feel the same? If only he could tell her.

She scooped a handful of sand and let the warm grains sift through her fingers.

Brett tugged on his earlobe. "That's how I found this gold earring. Maybe you'll find the mate."

She wasn't interested in finding any mate of anything.

He leaned back on his elbows, giving Andie a better view of his muscular chest. It seemed somewhere along the line; he had discovered the gym.

"Do you get out to the Key much?" she asked.

Brett sat back up. "Whenever I can. It's a good thing it's a state park, or you can bet he'd build condos all over it."

Andie's memory of Mike Austin was of a rough-edged businessman who loved big cars. But he was always nice to her and Jason. "He's still a developer?"

"Yep. He set me up with the restaurant as a last-ditch effort to get me off the wrong path. He's hands-off on the business side, though. That's on me." Brett smiled. "How about coming by for dinner? On the house."

"Eating out is a challenge with Sam, but I'll think about it." She dug her heels into the sand as guilt crept over her. She'd turned him down twice now. Once for a boat ride and now dinner. "Not that I don't appreciate your offer. But until this Draiocht is under control, I need to be careful where we go. Opening a garage door is nothing compared to other things he's done. No telling what's next."

Brett reached for her hand and squeezed it. The sudden touch of his hand broke Andie's thoughts.

"You aren't by yourself in Baga Shores. It's not as though we don't understand the joys of magical gifts," Brett said.

She pulled her hand away. "They're not always joys."

"True. How is Sam in school?"

"I so wanted him to fit into the Ordinary world." Andie shook her head. "But mainstreaming in a regular school didn't last." After Sam dropped the principal in a chair with a thud like a garage door. "He's been tested every way from Sunday. There's nothing physically wrong. We shelled out a ton of money to find out what I already knew. Intellectually, he's way above average for his age. He reads at a fifth-grade level. His math skills are fine. He writes words to tell us what he wants.

"Because of his high academic performance, we tried placing him in a school for gifted kids. It worked for a while until the administration, all Ordinaries, couldn't cope with Sam's unpredictability.

That was the final straw for his father, and he walked out. I've been homeschooling him for a year. But Sam needs more than just me."

Brett made circles in the sand with a stick. "I remember when my Draiocht started. I was younger than Sam. My body itched all the time. They say it's from the impulses stirring inside."

"Sam had the same problem. I tried creams and powders. I took him to an Ordinary doctor, but I couldn't tell the man the whole story. All he did was prescribe antihistamines, which didn't work. Sam seems better now."

"My mom might tell you how long the itching lasted for me." Brett sniffed a laugh. "After that, the Draiocht started."

Andie tried to hide a laugh. "Oh, I remember what a pistol you were."

"Yeah, well. Let's forget that. It wasn't long until I ended up in Rosemont," Brett said.

"Oh, God. Rosemont Academy. What a trip! Poor Mimi had such high hopes the place would help Jason and me. She imagined I'd graduate summa cum laude in witchery. That did not, will not, and won't ever happen."

"Rosemont doesn't award honors, Andie."

"Sam could never fit in there. Besides, they want you to grow the gift. I don't want that for him."

"Have you ever considered what he'd want?"

"Since he can't talk, I often assume what he does or doesn't want. I guess I've become a little overprotective, especially since his father left us."

"I was sorry to hear your marriage didn't work out." The sincerity in his eyes almost made her cry. If she started the tears now, she might not stop.

Andie drew her knees to her chest and swallowed the lump in her throat. "Sometimes we need to make mistakes to learn from them."

Why did she run her mouth like that? Brett Austin didn't care about her life history.

"We should go back. I don't want Sam to wear out my mother."

"Andie." The way he said her name wrapped her heart in warmth. *Hold on.* This was ridiculous. Home half a day and sitting alone on the beach with a man?

"Never mind." He stood first and offered his hand to help her up.

"About the boat ride. If you still mean it, how about tomorrow?" she asked. "Unless you have other plans?"

He let go of her hand. "I have something early in the morning."

Andie's heart crashed. Her pity-party confession had turned him off.

"I'm good after that, though. How about we take off around eleven-thirty? Think Sam would like the Key?" He flashed a sexy smile.

Her heart soared again. "It's a date."

Crimson fire spread across her cheeks as she looked down at her feet. This was not an official date. Especially not with the irritating brat who used to yank her hair.

She quivered at how hard he'd do it and how horribly it hurt.

No. This would be a field trip for Sam. Not a date.

AFTER BEACH TIME was over and Brett and the dog left, Andie and Sam went upstairs and had their showers. While her little boy napped on his bed, Andie relished this quiet time, though the room's gaudy decor numbed her brain.

BEWITCHING ANDIE

Naturally, her phone chose that moment to buzz. She debated letting it go to voice mail, but her brother's number was on caller ID. She took the phone outside on the balcony deck and swiped the screen to answer.

"How's it going?" Jason asked.

"You'll never guess who showed up."

"Mother."

"You aren't the psychic one. How'd you know?"

"I called Mimi earlier." Jason cleared his throat. "How does the place look to you?"

"Beautiful as I remembered, except for my gross bedroom."

"Have you seen mine?" Jason laughed. "Listen. I have some time off coming up. Thought I'd fly into Tampa, then drive over for a visit."

Though his pilot schedule limited their time together, Andie always loved seeing her brother, and Sam adored him.

But why hadn't Jason mentioned visiting here the last time they talked? It didn't make sense but add that to the list of other coincidences. Like Brett and her mother's *coincidental* arrival. Was this a conspiracy? Were they planning some kind of intervention? Did everyone think she had to be treated like a helpless porcelain doll?

After the call ended, she slid beside Sam and gave him a soft kiss on top of his head.

When she first got engaged to Steven McCraig, Andie had innocently assumed she'd have a wonderful marriage. There'd be delightful children, and they would live everyday suburban life as a real family.

A typical happily ever after story.

And it was, for a while. Who could predict Sam would be a late bloomer? Usually, Draio children show signs at age five. For Sam, it was when he was about to turn seven. Then things spiraled out of control.

For a few short hours, Andie had stored all these thoughts away like winter clothes in spring. As if cued, a parade of worst-case scenarios flurried in her mind like a turning snow globe. So much to do to start this new life. Why couldn't this first day be a quiet reunion?

Why? Because Mimi was up to something. Rhea, Brett, and now a call from Jason. Too much for her to believe they were just happy *coincidences*.

Andie tiptoed from the bedroom and went on the hunt for her grandmother. Time to set things straight.

Chapter Four

Brett stood at the upstairs deck railing admiring how efficiently his staff handled the early-bird customers. This setup wasn't bad for a guy who had minored in business and majored in beach. Nobody to worry about except himself and a dog and keeping the Dockside Grille in the black, and no long-term relationships to tie him down.

He relied on his finely-tuned early warning system to alert him to emotional involvement tentacles. And that meant with Andie, too.

Jason's sister or not, she'd grown into a beautiful, desirable woman who deserved someone better. Mimi would have to find somebody else for her information-gathering. Andie had enough worries without him hanging around. Brett needed to cut bait and fast.

His phone flashed a weather alert for an early evening storm coming off the Gulf. Low-lying Baga Shores would transform into a water park, but Sabrina and the staff had rolled down the window coverings. They handled storms just fine.

"Wake up, sleeping beauty. Time for a quick beach run before it hits."

Rex bounced up, tail wagging at full mast.

Inside, Brett changed quickly and grabbed an apple on the way out the door. By the time they crossed the road to the beach, ink-black clouds were forming in the distance. The wind had picked up, and he figured the storm would hit in about twenty minutes. For now, the blue Gulf waters sparkled like a chest full of shimmering gems.

He squinted and reached around his neck for a nonexistent cord. Where did he put his sunglasses this time? Brett tossed his half-eaten apple toward the water. Once it landed, five scavenger gulls encircled it. "Fetch it, boy. Show them who's boss."

The fearless retriever broke into the coven, scattered the birds, snatched the core, and dashed back.

"Good job." Brett patted the dog's back. "You face your demons like a champ. Let's go, boy."

He reflected on how he didn't deserve this life as they ran together. Due to luck, or the lack of it, he'd been born an Austin and slipped sideways into the family fortune, and he was the only son who didn't care about the money.

Brett picked up speed as he jogged along the sand. His formidable warrior retriever matched his stride. Usually, a hard run relaxed him and helped clear his head. No such luck today.

Each footstep pounded more thoughts crowding for attention. Andie in a bathing suit. The way her eyes glistened in the sunlight. Her full lips close to his.

Lightning speared the water. His arm hair raised. Deafening thunder.

All the same damn sensations right before the Draiocht used to emerge.

Not this time.

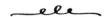

A PERSON CAN SET a clock by Florida afternoon storms. If Andie was safe inside, she loved to watch lightning dance over the Gulf. Every strike carried enough raw energy to destroy, yet it was mesmerizing. After a skull-jarring thunderclap shook the windows, she snapped the wooden bedroom blinds shut.

The boom had awakened Sam, napping in his bed.

"Let's go see what's happening downstairs," she said.

Hugging his backpack, the sleepy-eyed child followed Andie downstairs, where they found Mimi staring at the storm through the glass slider.

"Can we talk?" Andie asked.

Mimi gestured to the living room. Andie sat in the corner of the sofa and hugged a throw pillow. From here, she kept an eye on Sam at the breakfast bar.

"Andarta, I have a suspicion what this is about."

No use questioning Mimi's insight. "Brett's a nice guy, but I don't need a bodyguard."

"Dear child, he's not a bodyguard. He's a Draio. He can help prepare Sam for Rosemont."

Andie pounded her fists into the pillow. The puzzle pieces fit. No wonder her mother encouraged the walk along the beach with Brett. And why Brett soft-pedaled Rosemont yet failed to mention the part about him being expelled.

"Have you forgotten I went there?" Andie breathed out to the count of five. "It isn't set up for kids like Sam." She pressed two fingers on her forehead between her brows. Somebody once told her that would relieve anxiety. It didn't. "He doesn't belong in a place full of strangers." Andie cast her glance to the floor. "I thought between the two of us—"

"Don't you mean the three of us?" Tinkling bells drew Andie's attention to the other end of the sofa. Cross-legged, Rhea appeared with her cat curled in her lap.

Andie shook her head. "Can't you come into a room like an Ordinary?"

"How boring." Rhea cast a dismissive wave. "Anyway, what's wrong with the power of three? Your grandmother, me, and you."

Oh, sure. The power of three was potent and effective if all three witches were capable. "You both know I'm a failure at the craft."

"A few setbacks here and there doesn't mean failure, Andarta," Mimi said.

A few setbacks?

"Every time I cast a spell, the opposite intention happens. How about when I mix potions that turn to vinegar every single time?

"You think Mimi or I were perfect from the beginning? It took me years to refine this disappear-reappear thing."

"She's still not *purrrfect*."

Andie stretched her neck in the cat's direction. "It talks?"

The cat smirked, its golden-yellow eyes trained on Andie. "I prefer you call me Alika, thank you."

Familiars talked. Andie just hadn't heard one before. She certainly wasn't prepared to hear one that sounded like a middle-aged human male. Andie returned Alika's stare as he trotted across the room and jumped up on the stool next to Sam.

"Andarta?" Mimi's voice invaded Andie's trance.

Andie gave a long, audible sigh. "Any other surprises up your sleeves today?"

Rhea and Mimi exchanged amused glances.

"If you don't want Sam to go to Rosemont, then just what is your plan?" Mimi's sudden sharpness put Andie on the defensive.

"I don't want him to be magical. Or use magic. I want him to forget it."

"You might as well say you don't want a bird to use its wings. Or worse, you want to take their wings away," Rhea said.

"You don't understand." Andie's stomach balled into a knot. "The Draiocht will make his life impossible."

"For now, let's agree to disagree about that," Mimi countered. "Why do you feel this way about the magic you grew up with?"

"I used to believe it was good." Until Steven poisoned her with his beliefs and how using the Draiocht had made Sam's life miserable.

"It still is good, granddaughter. We can make this work, but it takes all three of us." Mimi stood and offered one hand to Andie and the other to Rhea.

"For my great-grandson," Mimi said.

Rhea extended a hand to Andie. "For my grandson."

The Draiocht might be a way for Sam to cope with his lack of verbal skills. Yet to Andie, Sam seemed content in his inner world. If she took their hands to affirm her family heritage, it would also compromise her belief that magic was inherently wrong. She could not do both.

Andie cast her glance at Sam. "I'm sorry. I just can't do this."

"Andarta, look at me," Mimi said.

Andie slowly brought her gaze back to meet her grandmother's stern countenance.

"The Draiocht magic is part of your inheritance through your grandfather to the old Celtic times. It is not to be forgotten, hidden, or misused. It is a God-given gift to cherish and protect. We are obligated to carry it forward for the betterment of man."

The same high and mighty story Andie had heard all her life.

Andie felt her blood go from simmer to boil. Why couldn't she make these women understand?

"To live in the Ordinary world, Sam must learn to function in it," Andie said.

"Piffle and nonsense!" Rhea huffed away to join Sam.

"Andarta, your biases will smother the boy!"

Andie's body quaked at the sound of Mimi's mighty voice.

"You were raised to believe our magic is not a belief or a religion." Mimi glanced at Sam and then back to Andie. "The heart and soul of a Draio shape the magic. That's why there are academies like Rosemont all over the world. They encourage the good in each child and cultivate the gift."

Andie bristled. "Sam is good."

Mimi gave Andie a radiant, calm smile. "Of course he is!" She swelled to her full height and unfolded her arms. "Look at us!"

Except Sam's lineage wasn't exclusively from Andie's grandparents. Indeed, half his genes came from Steven. Some came from her father, who she didn't know a thing about.

"Andarta, you've come out of a bad marriage to an intolerant Ordinary." Mimi's tenor softened. "Your views may be tainted for now, but I have faith in you and my grandson. You cannot raise this wonderful special child alone. The boy needs a mentor, so I asked Brett to be here when you arrived. To meet Sam. To test the waters, so to speak."

Andie chewed a hangnail. "I'm not crazy about outsiders working with Sam."

"Outsiders?" A glint of anger reflected in Mimi's eyes. "Well, I'm not crazy about my great-grandson being jerked around between the Ordinary world and ours."

Andie stared at the ceiling fan blades as they spun in endless circles. Thanks to her never-ending naivete, she had focused on coming back to Baga Shores. She hadn't put much thought into the "what then" part.

Joining with her mother and grandmother to create a powerful circle of three meant Andie must recommit to her craft. Something she was unwilling to do.

Andie fought to keep her temper. "It's no accident my mother is here. You summoned her."

"I wouldn't say summoned," Mimi said. "I prefer 'invited.' Don't underestimate the woman. She can be a great help."

"Yeah. Maybe, if she stays long enough. And what about Brett?"

Miriam shrugged. "I told you. Sam needs him."

Andie sharpened her gaze. "Is that your only motive?"

A cryptic grin bloomed on Mimi's face. And an uncomfortable heat flamed up Andie's neck. Allowing Brett to help with Sam meant she would be forced to spend time with him.

"Even if I agree to Rosemont, let's say, on a trial basis." Andie held up a finger to make a point. "It's too expensive."

Mimi waved the comment away as if Andie's words were annoying gnats. "Your grandfather set up a lovely endowment for Rosemont. Tuition is free for all students."

Andie had plodded deep into this discussion and was sinking fast. One last try. "I don't want my son to live there."

"Sam's age group attends day school three days a week. He wouldn't board there until he's older and only if the child and the family are ready. He needs competent training with a gift as powerful as I suspect his is. More than what Brett, you, or I could give the boy."

Andie looked toward the deck windows and at the darkening sky. It all seemed so rushed. She needed to get away from this conversation.

"I can't think about this right now. Would you keep an eye on Sam while I finish unpacking?" Andie asked.

"Of course. We shall bake cookies!"

Andie rolled her eyes. Grace's day off and associating her grandmother with anything domestic seemed farfetched.

"Mimi, since when do you bake cookies?"

"Since I learned how to open one of those tube things," Mimi said over her shoulder. "Rhea, my dear, do you know how to turn on the oven?"

What little Andie and Sam owned was in storage until she could find a place to live. She'd already put their things away, but the excuse gave her a few minutes alone to collect her thoughts.

She stood in the middle of the walk-in closet, empty except for one of Mimi's garment bags at the far end and what Andie'd already hung up: the denim skirt that needed re-hemming, a pair of white capris, one sundress, and her leather jacket.

A bare closet reminded her that nothing here was like it once was. The strangeness only intensified the dread that ground into Andie's bones. Though she'd lived in a loveless marriage for years, the divorce had upended her life. The daily changes in Sam frightened her. Niggling doubts popped up like weeds.

Was coming back here the right decision? She'd tried to raise him alone, but she couldn't get a job with the McCraig family working against her. She'd used up her meager savings. Child support payments barely covered expenses. So, where else could she go except back to Baga Shores?

With each new day, Sam's magic became stronger. He would overpower her soon now if he realized it.

And this whole Brett thing. Mimi must have primed him to tamp down his "Draio-ness." Any arrangement with Brett to work with Sam needed terms, conditions, and boundaries.

She'd talk to him about this as soon as she came up with something.

Her gaze caught on her guitar case. The instrument meant as much to her as Sam's markers and sketchbook did to him. Things each of them relied on for comfort.

A song returned to her as she lightly strummed through a few chords. One that had soothed a cranky baby Sam. She began humming the melody, then sang the lyrics she could remember.

It's a song just for me
When I see your face
Or say your name
Or hear your voice.
It's a song just for me.

She flattened her hand on the guitar strings. *Or hear your voice.* What she wouldn't give to hear Sam's voice.

She sang the song again, stopping before the last line. "Why can't I remember the end?" She shut her eyes to think.

Something rustled on the floor in front of her. Andie's eyes snapped open. Her mother was seated cross-legged in front of her, again with the black cat in her lap.

"Andarta, surely you remember I wrote this song for you when you were a baby."

With a lilting, fairylike voice, Rhea finished the song.

When you smile, I smile right back
And you laugh out loud
It's a song just for me.

Andie stiffened her back and leaned the guitar against the chair. She had no recollection of her mother singing to her.

"You sing beautifully," Rhea said. "Like an angel."

Andie was supposed to thank her mother for the compliment, but she was as mute as Sam.

"Tell me the truth." Rhea's eyes stared straight into Andie's heart. "Do you resent the magic because of me?"

What kind of question was that? How was she supposed to answer? *Oh, I forgive you, Mother, for disappearing weeks and months at a time. Let's hug and make up.*

Andie poked around her brain for a reply. "It's more complicated than that." An ambiguous truth.

"You and Jason are my jewels. I love you more than you can imagine." Rhea put her hand on Andie's and gave a gentle squeeze. "I could not commit to being the mother you two deserved."

Andie's fingers dug into her thigh as she fought the impulse to say something she shouldn't. In the awkward silence, Andie tried again to say the right thing. But nothing came out.

"Cookies are ready!" Mimi called from downstairs.

"Shall we?" Rhea asked.

"You go ahead. I'll be down in a few minutes."

Rhea started to leave, then turned around. "Oh, guess who figured out how to turn on the oven?"

Andie narrowed her gaze at Alika. "The cat?"

"Be serious. It was Sam. He turned it on like he'd done it a hundred times."

Andie chuckled. For a seven-year-old, Sam was pretty handy in the kitchen. But had he done it magically?

Rhea padded downstairs, but Alika remained with Andie. Clearly, the cat had something to say.

"Well?" Andie asked.

"She has much love for you and the boy. It is difficult for her to say so."

Alika's accent was unfamiliar.

"Does it matter where I'm from?"

A mind-reading cat to boot. "No doubt my mother found you on one of her trips," Andie said.

"To be accurate, I found her. She's quite remarkable if you would be kind enough to give her a chance. Now I have become tired of this conversation. I have said what I needed to say." Alika's tail flagged the air, and he disappeared.

Andie rolled her head until her neck crackled. "If anyone else in here feels compelled to give me advice, I have one word. Don't."

Chapter Five

Under the moonless sky, Andie sat in one of the deck chairs and sipped a Merlot. Their family dinner had been cordial and almost pleasant. Thankfully, Mimi hadn't mentioned Rosemont again.

She took another sip of the fruity wine. How wonderful would it be to have a home for her and Sam? One with a bright, sunny kitchen and an east window. A small patio for an herb garden like Mimi's.

She and Steven's house had been built for them as a wedding present from his father. It was nice, and she'd adjusted to it. But she'd had no input to the design or the furnishings. It never really felt like it was hers.

But having her own home required money, and that meant a job. Steven's support payments wouldn't be enough.

She laughed. For now, Mimi's home, with five bedrooms, a four-car garage, and a short walk to the water, would more than do.

The slider opened, and Sam joined her. The lounge chair had enough room for two. Andie tapped the space beside her.

"Remember our song?" The one the speech therapist suggested might help Sam speak.

Andie hummed the melody, then sang the words. "*I love you, now and ever, ever, more. I love you more than—*"

She waited with the hope he'd say something. Anything.

She threw in the first crazy word that came to mind. "*I love you more than cupcakes.*"

When that didn't work, she tried several more. Once again, Sam didn't finish one line of this song. Their impromptu music therapy session ended when he fell asleep with his head on her shoulder. She let him stay that way while she stared at the sky.

Despite her new doubts about coming home, she knew Sam was protected here. With Sam snuggled beside her, Steven's innuendoes that she was an unfit mother were distant and irrelevant.

When Mimi and Rhea joined them, they raised their glasses in a toast.

"To all four generations here at one time," Mimi said.

"To my delightful grandson," Rhea said.

"He's my life," Andie said as she hugged him.

Though she craved closeness with her mother, Andie still resented Rhea's gaps in her and Jason's lives. How could anyone go off and leave their children? What possible reason other than death? Or, like her ex-husband, disgust for his child.

She shifted her hips toward Sam to deliberately look away from her mother. Sam stirred, stretched, and accidentally punched Andie's chin.

"Okay, champ. Time for bed," she said as she rubbed her chin.

"May I?" Mimi asked.

Andie stiffened. She put the boy to bed almost every night of his life. "I should—"

Before she said another word, Sam jumped up and took Mimi's hand.

"Hey, where's my good-night kiss?" Andie asked.

Sam came back and gave her a quick peck on the cheek.

Once the slider shut behind Sam and Mimi, a screaming silence separated Rhea and Andie.

Long minutes passed before Rhea spoke. "He saw the cat and me before you did. Which magical gift does he have? Druids and Warlocks run in the family, you know."

Ordinary families talked about passing hair color and freckles from one generation to the next, not so in this family. Andie rubbed her jaw where Sam's fist had connected.

"He's a Draio," Andie whispered. "Like Jason."

"Are you serious?" Rhea clapped her hands. "No wonder Mimi was so excited. Do you realize how special it is that Jason and now Sam both have this gift? Our ancestors must be dancing a jig."

Rhea looked around as though expecting someone might be listening, then she cupped her mouth. "You have to be careful. They." She waved a hand around the air. "Draio's are sensitive to the proper titles. It is never wise to call a Draio a wizard," she whispered.

"I'll keep that in mind." Andie downed the rest of her wine. The last thing she needed now was to anger the dead. She had enough worries managing the living.

INSOMNIA HAD ONLY FUELED Andie's curiosity. Satisfied Sam was still burrowed under the covers in his bed; she wanted to see what else Mimi might have changed. Jason's old bedroom was across the hall. She tiptoed into it and flipped on the light.

Purple everywhere. Walls. Throw rugs. Bedspread.

Not a thing left that hinted a boy grew up here. Why had Mimi gotten rid of all evidence of their childhood? It didn't seem in keeping with her love of family.

Andie gave her mother's closed door a wide berth. There were two more bedrooms on this floor, always reserved for visiting family or Mimi's "guests." She stayed clear of those.

She hesitated at the stairs to the third floor. Would it hurt to peek in her apothecary if her grandmother was asleep?

She tiptoed up the stairs like a sneaky child, avoiding the seventh step that always squeaked. At the top, two plug-in nightlights illuminated the otherwise pitch-black hall.

When she was a kid, this hallway seemed like the longest corridor in the world. At the end was Mimi's apothecary. No one went into that room without Mimi, and there were no exceptions.

Though she and Jason had lived here for years, Andie had been invited inside only three or four times. Everyone respected Mimi's particular room.

Andie stopped at the door but couldn't bring herself to try the doorknob. What would she gain by going in?

Andie didn't know a magical stone or crystal from a plain rock and had no business in there. Yet an odd whirring noise intrigued her.

The door opened on its own. Andie slapped her hands to her chest and skipped back.

"You're more than welcome to join me," Mimi said from inside.

"I'm sorry." Andie's words hiccupped. "I didn't mean ... to bother you. I remember the rules. I couldn't sleep. I'll leave. No worries."

"Come in, dear."

Trembling, Andie barely kept her balance as she crossed the threshold. Mimi, her back to the door, arranged bottles on a shelf. She waved over her shoulder for Andie to enter.

Andie took a deep breath, inhaling hints of rosemary and lemongrass. She swallowed and took a cautious step forward while scanning the room.

Across the back were the familiar shelves full of small bottles and jars filled with oils and potions. Rows of dried herbs hung from a ceiling beam. What was with all those sealed shipping boxes?

The door clicked shut behind her, and Andie swiveled toward it. "Who did that?"

Mimi laughed as she waved her hand over a wall sensor to open, then shut the door. "I love technology."

Andie took it all in. LED lighting. Three computer screens. A computer printer whirring away. This was more like a strategic command center than a witch's apothecary.

"I want you to smell this new blend." Mimi held out a jar. "Tell me if you think there's too much rosemary."

Andie took a sniff. "Umm. It's perfect."

The printer beeped behind them. "Oh, damn. Be a dear and reload the tray. The mailing labels are in the top drawer," Mimi added. "Please pay attention to which way is up. I hate when I run them through upside down."

Quite possibly, Andie had drifted into sleep, and this was all a dream. What other explanation could there be? Dream or not, the printer wouldn't stop the annoying beep. Andie reloaded the tray and pressed the resume button. Its hunger satisfied, the printer continued cranking page after page.

Andie studied one of the computer screens divided into several live camera images. Inside the garage. At the front and back entrances. Around the house and on the deck. And the third-floor apothecary door.

So that's how Mimi knew she was out there.

Andie took a finished sheet from the tray. These were addresses for locations all over the world.

"Mimi?"

"Quite simple, my dear." She pressed a key to start another print run. "They're for my business."

"I'm sorry. What did you say?" The noisy printer must have masked Mimi's last words.

A proud smile broadened Mimi's face as she opened her arms. "You are standing in the middle of Potions with a Pop."

Andie plopped into the task chair. Upon impact, the chair rolled backward into a stack of empty shipping boxes that cascaded over and around Andie. She hurriedly gathered them into neat piles.

"You sell your potions?" Andie asked.

"My financial guru suggested it. He was right. This has turned into a nice supplemental revenue stream," Mimi said.

"You handle all this by yourself?" Andie asked.

Mimi cocked her head in Andie's direction. "I have given some thought to having a partner. Interested?"

"Me? You're joking. With my bad luck in the magic department?"

"Dear child, the power lives inside you and always has. It's like a little seed that needs proper rain and sunshine to break through the ground. You just need to get out of your own way and allow the gift to grow."

Andie muffled a laugh at her grandmother's sweet analogy. But she knew any tiny seed trying to grow inside her had rotted years ago.

Chapter Six

Despite the crick in his neck, Brett had faith that caffeine would be the miracle cure he needed right now.

Sleeping straight through a night had escaped Brett long ago. After another long session playing catch-up on the late quarterly business report, he'd given in to fitful napping on the sofa in his downstairs office.

Shortly after sunrise, he went up to his apartment and laser-focused on the pot of leftover coffee. He poured a cup and put it in the microwave.

Toting a bucket of rattling cleaning tools, Grace came around the corner from the bathroom. "Don't drink that!"

He jolted and slammed the oven door shut.

"You scared the crap out of me!" Brett forgot it was Grace's day to clean the apartment. "What's wrong with this coffee?"

Grace dumped the liquid down the sink. "It was there when I got here."

The brew was at least two days old. What a waste to throw it out, though.

Grace clucked her tongue. "Sometimes, you act like you don't have a dime to your name. Why don't you get one of those pod coffee makers?"

Brett yawned and raked his hand through his hair. "Coffee pods are expensive."

Grace rolled her eyes as she made a new pot. While it brewed, Brett filled Rex's dish. The dog gyrated in a half-sway, half-wiggle accompanied by a throaty yelp.

"Is that hula dance for me or the chow?" he asked.

Oblivious, the dog vacuumed the food bits and slurped from his water dish.

"Guess I got my answer," Brett said.

"You realize you just got conned into giving him a second breakfast?" Grace frowned. "Where'd you sleep last night, or am I too nosy?"

"Cool your jets." He massaged his neck. "In the office. Alone."

"You slept on that ratty couch downstairs?" Grace cast a "whatever" wave.

Brett had spent half the night watching movies and the rest of the time on that quarterly report until his eyes crossed. Why would he bother going upstairs when the sofa was right there?

"It is not ratty." Maybe a crack or two in the leather, and one side sagged—a lot.

"Humph. Matter of opinion." Grace admired her reflection on the stainless-steel refrigerator she'd buffed to a shine. "Perfect."

The coffee was perfect, not a shiny door. The strangled trickle better fill the pot soon, or he wouldn't be accountable for his actions. Screw it. He slid the container out with Olympian reflexes, filled his cup, and slid it back without losing a drop.

"Honestly, Brett Austin. Sometimes I don't understand you."

"Because I reheat coffee?"

Brett needed a housekeeper like a third foot, but Grace needed work. On her off day from Mimi's, Grace picked up hours at Brett's.

"How are your classes going?" he asked.

Grace shrugged. "It can be tricky with children and a job."

"Met any eligible men?"

"Not hardly!" Grace fisted the cloth she carried. "Nobody will ever replace Manny. Besides, I'm twenty years older than most people in my classes. Who wants somebody with a built-in family?"

It was his fault Grace needed two jobs. If it weren't for him, Manny would still be alive. Along with one day a week working for him, Brett paid Grace's tuition. It was the least he could do.

"The right man's out there," Brett said softly.

As it would be for Andie and her built-in family. But it wasn't him.

He took the half-and-half from the fridge, careful not to press a fingerprint on anything but the door handle. He sniffed the open container and scowled. "This expired two weeks ago."

"Imagine that," Grace said. "I'll clean out the fridge before I leave. What did you think of Andarta?"

Bookkeeping hadn't been the only thing that kept him awake. Andie was a gorgeous woman. Brett was almost ashamed of his attraction to her. Almost. He needed to take the high road and fight his instincts.

He might help her where he could, but he would not get entangled in her business or her sheets.

"Brett? You didn't answer the question." Grace began inspecting refrigerator contents and throwing away spoiled items.

"She's grown up since I last saw her." Grown-up a lot.

"Miriam has high hopes for the boy," Grace said.

"She wants me to work with him."

"No better person," Grace said.

Two years ago, he might have been the right person to help Sam. If

...

If the Draiocht hadn't failed.

If he'd saved Grace's husband, the best mentor Brett ever had.

Th *if* that hauled memories by the bucketload. The flare from the gun barrel. The eardrum-splitting blast. Chasing and losing the bungling punk robber. Holding Manny in his arms.

Until he died.

"I need to walk Rex." Brett took the dog outside to the deck. From here and facing east across the Intercoastal, he could see the Tampa skyline that etched the horizon. On the west, the Gulf of Mexico. Who wouldn't love this life?

"Let's go, boy."

Halfway down the stairs, someone yelled his name from inside the restaurant. *God bless America. Not now.*

He straddled the threshold between the indoor and outdoor dining areas.

"Brett. Stop right there." Kelly was the latest in a string of Dockside managers since Manny's murder. The calamity magnet's shrill voice stung his ears and carried across the county.

"What is it?" he asked.

"We have to talk." Kelly slumped into a chair, her fingers splayed across her chest.

"What's wrong this time?"

Brett glimpsed Sabrina with her palms in an "I give up" gesture.

"The produce company," Kelly panted. "They can't deliver today. You know what this means?"

Nuclear attack? Tsunami surge? The apocalypse?

"Enlighten me," he said.

Kelly shot him an "are you kidding" smirk. "No lettuce. That's what it means. No tomatoes. No carrots. No onions. Nothing. How do you expect me to run a kitchen like this?"

"Uh, Kelly. We don't open for another three hours. Try another supplier."

"Me?" She leaned forward and wagged her finger at Brett. "This is not my restaurant. Furthermore, you can shove this job where the sun doesn't shine. I'm out of here."

Brett shut his eyes and inhaled the deepest breath his lungs could handle. He let it out slowly, counting backward from ten.

He opened his eyes and glanced to the front door, where Sabrina stood, holding a bike helmet.

Kelly stormed across the room, snatched the helmet, and blew through the doorway.

"Don't let the screen hit you where the good lord split you," he muttered.

Sabrina sat on a barstool next to Brett. In quiet meditation, they stared at the rows of colorful liquor bottles lined up on shelves behind the bar. Neither said a word until they were sure Kelly had pedaled far, far away.

"So?" he asked.

Sabrina flashed a Zenlike smile. "I already called our backup distributor."

"And?"

"Here, within the hour."

"You're the best. I've been thinking. How'd you like a promotion? It seems I have an opening."

"Ohhh. Noooo. I'm not cut out for this."

"I have faith in you." Shit. He sounded like Mimi and Grace. But it was the truth for Sabrina.

Brett checked the time. He'd stop by Baga Bagels, then take the boat up to Miriam's. "Can you handle things here?"

"You're supposed to meet with the accountant this morning. Did you forget?"

Forget? No. Want to? No, again. "I'll call and reschedule. The numbers are off, Sabrina. The report's not ready. I should have let you take it from the start."

"I'll make the call." She headed toward Brett's office. "Tell Miriam I said hello."

"How'd you know?"

"Lucky guess. Remember what I told you. Something's brewing."

How could he forget?

Chapter Seven

Wrapped in sleep's cobwebs, Andie rolled on her side.

It had been months since she'd slept this late. Her eyes fluttered open to discover Sam's empty bed. Her heart pinched as she bolted to the balcony door. Still locked, thank God. Where did he go?

"The boy's downstairs with the others." Out of nowhere, the cat appeared in the middle of Sam's bed, casually grooming.

Andie released a deep breath. How long had that cat been in here?

"Mere moments."

Reluctantly, she'd accepted the thing's ephemeral nature. His mind-reading drove her crazy.

"Do not worry." He clawed the back of his ear. "I have more important things to do than spend time reading your confused mind. I am not assigned to you, only to your mother. I can turn it off. Would you prefer that I do?"

She cast him a narrow stare. "What do you think?"

He spat out a clump of fur. "This does not present a problem for me. Consider it done."

"Whoopie for you."

"Your attitude does nothing to solve your dilemma. I believe that you have not made your decision about the boy. To influence you would be presumptive on my part."

"Yes, it would. The *boy's* name is Sam."

"I am aware. *My* name is Alika."

"Point taken."

"My studied conclusion is that you must accept your grandmother's advice. Join them. There is value in the mighty three."

"Well, thank you so very much."

"Indeed, I detect sarcasm that I will not honor with appreciation. I only offer advice based on my many years of consorting with your species."

"Consorting? Exactly what do you mean by *species*?"

"Come now. Must I take these words to pen and paper and write them out for you?" He held up a paw. "Though I am not sure how I would do such a thing. The term humans use to describe us is familiar, yes? Call us anything you want. We are duty-bound to walk beside our chosen one, even stay a few steps ahead. I must say, with your mother, it is wise to stay many steps ahead. We see pitfalls before humans do, and we help avoid them."

"You are not my familiar."

"True. I am your mother's. What is of concern to her concerns me as well."

Andie's attention was drawn downstairs and Brett's distinctive voice. She thought he was busy this morning. The boat ride wasn't until eleven-thirty.

"And in the name of all things you treasure in this realm, let that man help your son."

Alika disappeared into the ether. Andie, still in her pajamas, went downstairs.

Dressed to the nines, Mimi was in full makeup with her silver hair swirled into a gold clip.

She held up a bag. "Andarta, look what our angel Brett brought us. Baga Bagels. Be a dear and make us coffee "

Brett's wide smile filled her with joy. What joy? Remembering her new rule about men, she needed to know the guy *before* letting those feelings arise.

She stepped around Rex and Sam, playing tug-of-war with a dog toy. As she attempted to fill the coffee maker, her shaking hands spilled more water on the counter than she poured into the machine.

"Can I help?" Brett took a paper towel and wiped the counter.

"Guess I'm not quite awake."

Brett took over making coffee. "Do me a favor?"

She tilted her head toward him. "Favor?"

"Next time you see Grace, make sure she knows I fixed fresh coffee."

"Sounds like there's a story there," she said.

He stood inches away, silently staring at her with deep brown eyes. Why didn't he move or say something?

"Cups are behind you," he said.

"Cups? Oh, right." She stepped to the side as he reached into the cabinet. When his arm brushed her shoulder, she noted his slightly musky scent. Another blast of heat rose to her neck at how she was turned on by it.

Her brain fog cleared, and Andie busied herself getting plates and silverware.

They crisscrossed the kitchen until a miscue, and they bumped hips. Their self-conscious "excuse me's" overlapped.

One of them should move.

Brett's warm hand grazed her back. His fingertips lingered, causing a tickling sensation across her chest.

Not that? She glanced down.

She had not brushed her teeth yet, but she'd also forgotten she was still wearing pajamas. She threw a dishtowel over her shoulder, kidding herself that it would cover her chest.

"Be right back." She took the stairs two at a time, went into her bedroom, and put on her bra, a shirt, and shorts. She took a few extra minutes to brush her teeth and gather her hair into a ponytail.

She spun to dash downstairs, and with a gasp, she nearly tripped over Rex, positioned in the doorway.

"You could have knocked." She scratched under his chin. "You are a good boy, Rex. Thank you for making Sam happy. I haven't been very nice to you. I'm sorry."

The dog sneezed and shook his body, which Andie took as "apology accepted."

Downstairs, no one seemed to notice her wardrobe change, thank goodness. She touched her finger to her lips in an *Shh* to Rex, who cocked his head to the side and lay by Brett's feet.

Impossible to tell around here which animals talked and blabbed secrets.

Intent on her clothes, she realized Brett had on the same shirt and shorts as yesterday. Had he spent the night with someone else? *Stop it! It's nobody's business what the man did with his life.*

This was a Saturday morning she'd always imagined. While her family, though dysfunctional, bustled around, a beautiful kitchen unfolded in her mind. It wouldn't be as glamorous as Mimi's, but as long as it was all her own, who cared?

Once the coffee finished, everyone found a place at the breakfast bar. Andie slathered maple cream cheese on a cinnamon bagel, only to have her first bite interrupted by someone's phone chime.

She and Brett checked theirs at the same time.

"Not me," Brett said.

Andie stared at her screen and went numb. She went outside, shutting the door behind her.

"Hey, baby." Steven McCraig's voice ripped a chunk from Andie's heart.

How did he get this new number? Why didn't she let this call go to voice mail?

"Baby, you still there?" Steven asked.

The word *baby* nauseated her. Yes, still there. For a long time. "What do you want?"

"I didn't realize how much I'd miss you and Sport."

Did he think she was a moron? She hated how he kept calling their son 'Sport.' And the absentee husband and father missed them? Barefoot on the last step before the sand, she tightened an arm across her midriff.

"We have an agreement." Andie measured each word. Steven had abandoned them and blown any chance to spend more than a few supervised hours with Sam. "Nothing's changed. Once a month. My lawyer will set up something with yours on the location."

"How about down there in Baga Shores?"

"How did you know I was here?" Her gut cramp worsened.

"Where else would you go but back to those people?" His vitriol oozed through the phone.

"You mean my friends and my family?" she said through gritted teeth.

"Sam's my son. I still have rights. Especially now."

Especially now? Fear coiled around her throat with python strength.

Still barefoot, she stepped into the sand and was rewarded by a renegade Australian pine nettle implanted smack in the center of her arch. The intense pain knifed through her.

"Owwweeow," she yelled.

She pulled the burr from her foot, wishing the man on the phone was as easy to extract from her life. "I'm done talking to you. My attorney will be in touch."

"Andie, wait. Divorce was wrong. I know that now." He slithered into sweet talk. "Do we need a lawyer every time we discuss our son? Is this how it will be for the rest of our lives?"

Yes, if she had her way. "Steven, don't you dare go back over that again." And what's with his sudden change of heart?

"You can't hide him forever," Steven said.

Andie tightened a death grip around the phone. "We aren't hiding."

"Sam belongs with me." Steven's anger amped up. "With my family."

"Your family?" Andie choked on the words. "They'd destroy all that's good in the child."

Revulsion swept over her. Steven didn't care a whit about their well-being or any reconciliation. He wanted Sam back to save a few bucks in child support. Or even worse, was he going to exploit Sam's emerging Draiocht?

Or both?

Over her living or dead body, he would never get Sam back.

"You know the terms. You're lucky to get supervised visits," Andie said. "I'm warning you. Don't you dare try anything stupid." She ended the call, blocked the audacious jackass's number, and sat down on the top step. The divorce had not been pretty. Though what divorce ever was?

She sat on the top step, wrapped her arms around her knees, and stared through the sea grape canopy to the water. This beautiful place. The cozy breakfast. The beach where Sam ran with the dog. Brett's generosity. All too good to be true.

Steven McCraig would not ruin this. He'd back off, or she'd sue him for harassment. The idea didn't bring her enjoyment, but it was satisfying.

Sam was old enough to understand why he had to control the magic. They would start today. She rose, brushed herself off, and turned.

Sam stood right behind her, his eyes brimming with tears.

Andie's stomach roiled. How long had he been there? No matter. He'd heard only Andie's angry words and none of Steven's half-baked rant.

Still seething after the phone conversation, Andie pecked around for the right thing to say. The wrong thing now would slash her baby's heart. Though Steven epitomized a loser, he was her son's father. Sam was the only good thing the man had ever produced in his life.

It dawned on her that Steven didn't ask to speak to Sam. Or even ask how he was doing. The manipulative bastard didn't give two cents about "Sport."

"Daddy said to tell you he misses you." Andie cringed at how easy that half-truth passed her lips.

Rex inched next to Sam, nudged his hand, and head-bumped his arm to draw the boy's attention. Sam and Rex walked back inside, dragging Andie's soul behind them.

Too gutted to follow, she slumped into a lounge chair, scarcely noticing Brett beside her, offering a cup of coffee. She took a sip and looked toward the living room, where Sam now sat on the floor next to Rex. Mimi sat on the sofa across from them.

"I should go to him," Andie said.

"Give him a few minutes," Brett said.

"How much did he hear?"

"He came outside when he thought something happened to you."

She rubbed her foot. "I stepped on a pine nettle."

Undoubtedly, Sam had heard what she tried hard not to discuss around him.

"I have a new number. How did Steven find it?" Her question was directed to no one.

"If you need to talk, people say I'm a good listener." His concerned look made her want to cry again.

Andie looked away from Brett and stared into her cup as Steven's words pummeled her. *Divorce was wrong, Andie.*

Strand by strand, the blame web spun around her thoughts. Was it her fault the marriage failed? Would more counseling have helped? Would staying with him have made a difference?

No. No. No, on all counts. She'd traveled that dead-end road too many times.

"I don't know what Jason already told you," she said.

"Not that much, Andie," he said.

She hugged her knees to her chest. If Brett sincerely wanted to help, he needed to know at least the part that concerned Sam.

"After Sam started showing the gift, we enrolled him in a different public school for a fresh start. Ordinary schools don't ask questions about magical gifts on the enrollment paperwork, and I sure the heck wouldn't volunteer it. We thought we'd convinced Sam that this new school was a no-magic zone. He's never been one to listen. Not even a week after he started there, we got a call from an irate parent. She claimed Sam had struck her son, knocking him into the air.

"Sam wouldn't hit anyone. Besides, he doesn't have to touch anything to move it. The child and his hideous mother were horrible people, so a tiny part of me cheered for Sam. When Steven found out, he exploded.

"Then other kids started daring Sam to do it again. All he wanted was to fit in. So when he did it *again* to the same kid, the school called us in. Steven, Sam, the principal, me, and a counselor sat around a large conference table.

"The stupid conversation went in circles. Nobody believed Sam lifted the kids. He must have physically attacked them. I tried to explain that Sam had special abilities."

"You didn't mention the Draiocht, right?" Brett asked.

"I couldn't. These people weren't Baga Shores Ordinaries who understand us. The counselor went back over the delayed speech thing, which frustrated Sam. When he'd had enough, Sam raised his hands like this." Andie mimicked Sam's gesture. "And he lifted the principal. Still in his chair, I might add."

Brett tried to hide a laugh. "How high?"

"It's funny now." Andie lifted her hand to shoulder height. "About like this."

"That high? You're kidding?"

"Not kidding. The entire time the principal hovered, he and Steven shouted at Sam to put the chair down. The counselor scooted herself back to the wall. In the chaos, I got Sam's attention and convinced him to put Mr. Sawyer down."

"Then?" Brett asked.

"You saw what happened with the garage door."

Brett laughed out loud and quickly stifled it. "He dropped him?"

"Like a rock. After that, hysterical gossip spread like a firestorm that Sam McCraig was possessed. That only validated Steven's opinion about Baga Shores and me. Steven left us that day and sent his friends to get his stuff out of the house. Forty-eight hours later, the separation papers arrived."

She sipped her lukewarm coffee, then met Brett's soft gaze.

"Have you ever been married?"

He shook his head.

"You're lucky. It's hell when it ends."

Chapter Eight

The patio slider opened, and Rex and the boy bounded outside. Brett watched Andie call to Sam as he was about to take off for the beach. Brett couldn't hear her words when she knelt beside Sam, but he sensed her struggle. He didn't envy her the responsibility of raising this boy alone.

It took a lot of energy for his parents to raise three Draios. Andie's story brought it all back.

When he was a little younger than Sam, Brett had discovered how much fun it was to move things. A whole lot of fun at first. Moving his toys got old. By middle school, he'd graduated to more substantial items, like cows and cars, that tended to get him noticed and not in the right way.

Mimi stood in the doorway. "Now you understand?"

He understood too well.

Andie and Sam started back to the house. Brett hoped they'd worked through it.

Mimi held her hand out to Sam. "How about we split a bagel?"

Andie didn't follow them inside. Instead, she sat on a lounge chair. "I hate it, but I think Rosemont might be the only solution," she said.

"Does he know?" Brett asked.

She shook her head. "I've never talked about it with him. I needed to convince myself first."

Rosemont might be the right place for the wimps who wanted the magic controlled. Brett had bucked the system to the bitter end, proud of himself for being the school's class-A screw-up. Little Sam needed a mentor, but Rosemont?

She cast a long stare beyond the deck. "Mimi thinks you could help him."

Me? He was nobody's role model. Brett rode his dad's wealth like a surfer on a wave for most of his adult life. Truly a marvel that he'd survived those badass days.

Brett didn't know what to do first when his father bought the Dockside for him. Grace's husband, Manny, had taken Brett under his wing and taught him about business and about being a man. What did Manny Henderson get in return?

Dying in Brett's arms.

"I'm not the right person," he said.

"Others disagree." She stepped closer, kissed his cheek, and quickly stepped back. "Thank you for listening."

Only steely determination and respect for her situation kept Brett from making a move on her. How easy to tell her it would all work out. If only he felt it would.

Brett followed Andie into the kitchen. "Ahoy, sailor," he called out to Sam. "We shove off in fifteen minutes. Are you ready?"

"Upstairs and change into your swimsuit," Andie added, then turned to Brett. "You do have child-size life jackets, right?"

"Yes, Andie."

"You won't run the boat too fast, right?"

"I promise slow and safe."

"You're a good swimmer, right?"

"Come on, worrywart." He reached toward her ponytail.

She flashed a tiny smile as she ducked. "Hold it! I'm not that little bony-kneed kid anymore. I can defend myself now. So don't even think about it!"

Too late for that. Andie was all he thought about.

A GORGEOUS PEARL-WHITE cruiser was moored in Mimi's private dock across the street. Andie's fears about Sam falling overboard dropped a few degrees.

"This is yours?" Andie asked.

"One hundred percent." Brett climbed on board.

Faster than she could react, her son straddled the space between the bobbing boat and the dock. Andie's breath hitched at how fast he got away. But Brett had Sam around the waist and lifted into the boat before she exhaled.

Next, Brett's warm hand pressed into her lower back as he steadied her into the boat. It was a sweet gesture that tugged her heart and ignited a spark of desire.

As he slid the ropes off the moorings, Andie stole a look at his well-built body. There wasn't an ounce of extra flesh on his frame. All solid. All man. He hit all the right physical notes.

Time out! She wasn't on this ride to satisfy some romantic fantasy. The excursion was purely for Sam. *Right?*

Steven was a good-looking man, too. In the beginning, he made her feel like she was the only woman in the world. Bit by bit, his fake exterior chipped away until all that was left was a selfish man full of bigoted hate.

Andie snapped back to the moment. Sam had just bolted toward the bow and Rex. What was with this impulsiveness?

"Where do you think you're going?" She snagged him by the elastic in his trunks, scooted him back to his seat, and adjusted his life jacket. She tucked her hat brim under her thigh. She wasn't about to lose it again.

Sam pointed to her life jacket. So he was mothering the mother, eh? She fastened her straps and settled back in her seat next to Brett's. Brett idled through the no-wake zone with Rex in position as the figurehead. Sam's second attempt to join Rex was aborted when Andie caught him again.

Sam sat with a thud.

"Only four-legged passengers allowed on the bow," Brett called. "That's the rule."

Andie mouthed "thank you" back to Brett, who responded with a smile.

"Twenty minutes to the pass. We'll go out on the open water from there," Brett said.

With Sam settled, she relaxed and stole another glance at Brett, carefully navigating the boat. His striking features had softened, and though sunglasses hid his eyes, a subtle smile teased his lips.

Yesterday, she and Sam had left their home toward an uncertain future. Now they cruised the Intercoastal toward the pass to the Gulf of Mexico. A boulder the size of Alabama rolled off her shoulders. More layers of doubt peeled away. Her decision to come home was the right one. It wouldn't always be smooth sailing on calm waters, but she felt better about overcoming anything. Even Steven's ridiculous claims.

They cruised a while longer before Brett gestured to the right. "My place."

Andie peered over her sunglasses. Did he own the old Dockside? She remembered it as a run-down dive bar. From here, it looked fresh and friendly. Brett sounded the horn, and diners' cheers and waves greeted them.

Once they entered open waters, memories flooded back of being on her grandfather's boat with her family of aunts, uncles, and cousins. Those dear people had filled the gap left by her mother's sporadic visits.

That good feeling carried over to Brett at the helm. With Sam finally settled, Andie relaxed after the emotional roller coaster of Steven's phone call. She tipped her head back and let the wind and salty sea spray have their way with her.

Soon, she sensed that Brett had slowed the cruiser and idled offshore.

"Sam, that's Mimi's house," Brett said.

Mimi Tanner's impressive home, built to withstand hurricanes, stood out from all others along the water. Built at a time before Baga Shores accepted magicals, the house served as a supportive compound for Mimi and her husband's large family.

Andie shivered despite the warm breeze coming off the water. The house and Mimi were inseparable. What would happen to the place after her grandmother was gone?

Jason traveled and wouldn't be interested in taking it over. Rhea couldn't. Andie's aunts and uncles, and their kids, were scattered all over the world.

If Andie found a job on this side of the bay, she could share the home with Mimi. Then Sam could live the life he deserved all the time.

But with Sam in Rosemont as a day student, she had to live near the Tampa campus. Sam was her priority, so she'd do whatever she had to. For now, Mimi was strong and healthy, as was her home.

Brett turned the boat toward the Key. Soon they pulled into a four-slip dock. The beach was quiet except for water lapping against the boat and a few buzzing bugs. The building with the snack and bait shop was closed.

"All ashore." Brett extended his hand.

She tapped her hat down tight, took his hand, and climbed on the dock. Brett repeated the gesture with Sam, retrieved a beach bag, and slung it over his shoulder. Rex had disembarked and was trotting ahead.

"Rex knows the place up ahead on the west side." Brett led them to the spot and spread a blanket in the shade of a palm tree.

Lemon Key's panoramic view of the vast Gulf was as fantastic as she'd remembered.

She took sunscreen from Brett's bag, slathered Sam's arms and little-boy chest, and smeared a stripe across his nose. "Now you're ready."

They left their flip-flops, her cover-up, and hat beside the blanket and followed a flock of sandpipers skittering ahead. At the water's edge, she held Sam's hand as they went out to where the water covered his knees. Brett had pulled off his T-shirt and joined them.

He took Sam's other hand. "If it's okay with your mom, we can swim here," Brett said.

Brett's firm bare chest and arms were evidence that he was certainly capable. Sam was a reasonable swimmer. The water was quiet. But it meant she had to let go of her son and trust him to Brett.

While she dithered, Brett had swum a few yards out, dived down, and reemerged. His broad, naked, wet chest glistened in the sun when he raised his hands to run his fingers through his hair.

Was it Sam or herself that she couldn't trust around Brett?

"Honey, do you think you can swim out to meet him?" she asked.

Sam splashed into the water and started dog-paddling beside Rex.

"Be careful!" she called as she paddled out to join them. She treaded the warm water and watched Brett's strong arms support Sam.

When Brett let Sam swim on his own, her heart froze. Could Sam do this? What if a rogue wave hit them? As Sam maneuvered around Rex and Brett and back to her, her fears turned to delight.

Sam hugged his arms around Andie's neck and gave her a salty kiss on the cheek.

"Love you too, honey. Having fun?"

Sam broke his hold and swam back to Brett. He made the circuit ten times before he seemed tired. She motioned to Brett to go back to the beach.

Before Brett had left his apartment, Grace had packed them a lunch consisting of cheese, crackers, grapes, and smoked ham. Mimi had added a bag of sugar cookies from last night that were surprisingly good.

After he'd eaten, Sam laid his head in Andie's lap and fell asleep. Brett retrieved two single-serving wine containers from the bag.

"Grace thought of everything," Andie said.

"Allow me." Brett peeled off the seal.

Andie took a sip and scanned the shoreline.

"Can you believe this island didn't exist before the hurricane hit in the 1800s? It looks like it's been here forever," she said.

"The big blows are like that. Roll in, destroy what they can, and roll on." He leaned back on his elbows. "Sometimes, what's left is better."

"I hope that's true for my life." Andie ran her fingers over Sam's hair. "I hate being so suspicious, but there's so much at stake. I can't be with him every day for the rest of his life. I don't know how to keep this up as it is."

He removed his sunglasses and stared into her eyes. "Thinking like that plays right into your ex-husband's plan. As I said before, there's a whole community willing to support you."

She steeled her jaw to fight tears. Brett might be correct, but as she'd explained to Mimi, bringing outsiders into her problems was off the table.

She could have stayed on this tiny island forever, but they had to get back. Too soon, Mimi's dock was in sight. Brett helped Andie off the boat, but Sam wouldn't budge.

"Honey, we need to let Brett go home," she said.

Sam shook his head wildly, and Andie braced for another of his meltdowns. She hadn't anticipated this reaction.

"Sorry, Sam. You're Mom's right," Brett said.

Sam let Brett lift him out but made a pouty lower lip large enough to trip over.

Andie shot Brett an exasperated glance.

"Remember what I said about asking for help," Brett said.

She untied the last dock line and tossed the rope to Brett. "I appreciate the offer. But I got this."

Chapter Nine

It had been five days since Andie entered the apothecary, and she'd steered clear since then. It made her a nervous wreck, fearing any minute she'd knock into some exotic blend and ruin some one-of-a-kind recipe.

But her grandmother had insisted she come up today. Wise people obeyed Mimi. The door opened, and Andie cautiously stepped inside.

Mimi sat at the computer. "Come here."

Andie looked over her grandmother's shoulder, impressed with the woman's computer fluency as she bounced through different screens.

"There." Mimi sat back, sporting a self-satisfied grin. "What do you think?"

Andie furrowed her brow. Why did her grandmother want her to see an empty storefront?

"I don't understand," she said.

"I've been negotiating with the owner for weeks. Just this morning, we agreed to terms."

"Terms to what?"

Mimi held up a document. "To a lease."

"A lease to what?" Andie was no better mind reader than she was a good witch.

"This is the new Potions with a Pop retail shop in Baga Shores. I can sell and ship from there. No more stacks of boxes in here. No more trips to the post office or parcel shipping office. They'll pick up right at the store. Aren't you excited?"

Andie slanted her gaze away from the screen and around the room. "You're moving all of this?"

"Heavens no. Only sales and shipping in the shop. The preparation stays here. Isn't it wonderful?"

Somehow Andie couldn't picture her grandmother hustling sales. But who was she to burst the bubble? "Retail is tough work. You have someone in mind to help run it?"

Mimi sat up straight. "Why, Rhea, of course."

Andie glanced at the second computer screen with the security images. Rhea and Sam sat at the table having lunch on the back deck.

"Uh, you sure about Mother? I mean, she might not be the most reliable worker around."

"She and I have discussed this. Your mother is tired of vagabonding—my word, by the way. She loves the idea."

"Are you?" Andie couldn't stifle her giggle. "Kidding?"

Her subsequent laughs were soundless, deep, soul-scrapers until a roar erupted along with laughter tears.

"Are you through yet?" Mimi asked.

"I'm sorry. But the visual of my mother ..." Another hysterical wave of laughter came over Andie. "My mother staying in one place? In all her forty-six years, she's never had a job that I know of."

"Enough!" Mimi turned from the computer to Andie. "I take my daughter's word seriously."

"Okay, okay. But I think you might want more help than just my mother." Andie shrunk back a bit at Mimi's severe stare. "You know? Just in case?"

"I already thought of that." Mimi stood erect in full matriarch mode.

Andie took a quick look over each shoulder. Had one of Mimi's time-traveling guests arrived? The ghost of Henry Ford? Or Andrew Carnegie? *Somebody who could run this business from the grave and not into the grave as her mother might.*

Andie returned her grandmother's gaze with a cold, sober stare. "Don't be funny, Mimi."

"Who's being funny? My dear, I love you and Sam as much as any of my other children, grands, and greats. I am always here for each of you. But there will come a time when I'm not around."

"Don't talk like that."

"All this—" Mimi's hand swept the air around the room. "All this must not die with me. I need you to take it forward."

Wait? What? She needed who to take it forward?

"Ahhh, no. Remember me? The klutzy witch?"

"Andarta, all you need is more practice." Mimi shuffled through some cabinets and retrieved a small, carved wooden box. "And this."

Andie's gaze narrowed as she regarded the box with wonder and, simultaneously, with a touch of dread. "What's that?"

Mimi reached her hand forward. "Open it and see."

Andie took the box, handling it like a newborn kitten. She ran her finger around the ornately carved designs on the lid, rubbed smooth from many generations doing the same thing. She looked up at her grandmother.

"Go on," Mimi said.

Not knowing what might fly out, Andie held the box at arm's length, and after she jiggled the top, the tenacious lid opened. Inside was a velvet pouch.

She tipped the contents into her palm. Out slipped a beautiful, multifaceted triangular amethyst the size of a half-dollar coin hanging on a gold chain. Andie held the polished stone up to an LED lamp. Each cut reflected a hundred rays of light.

"Watch this." Mimi turned off the lamp, and the stone continued to radiate.

"I don't understand," Andie said.

"There are only three like this in the world. The one in your hand ..." Mimi reached around her neck and pulled up an identical one tucked inside her blouse. "This one."

"Who has the third?" Andie asked.

Mimi tapped the security camera view of the deck.

She had to be kidding. "Mother?"

"Now be a dear and put it on." Mimi folded the lease document into an envelope. "I promised to get this back today. Could you drop it off at the new store? And if you would, please stop by the market on your way back." Mimi handed her the envelope and a grocery list.

"Mimi, aren't you forgetting something?"

"Oh, of course. Charge the groceries to my account."

"No. I mean this." Andie held up the necklace.

"Yes. Yes. Go ahead and put it on, and we'll talk later." Mimi checked the time. "Now scurry along."

"Wait a minute! Could you give me something to go on here? What happens when—I mean *if*—I put this on?"

"It's going to rock your life," Mimi said with a bright smile.

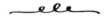

THOUGH OFFERED TO BABYSIT SAM, Andie brought him along as she ran Mimi's errands. She wore the necklace to humor her grandmother. Still, she tucked it under her shirt so that nobody could see it. She'd darn sure get some answers later about this thing. Why hadn't she ever seen Mimi's or Rhea's before?

Andie met the store owner at the shop and took a walk-through. It seemed like a prime location with plenty of parking—even some built-in shelves but not enough for Mimi's inventory. The walls could use a coat of paint.

While she was with the owner, Andie wondered if he was a *friend* like Grace. Did he understand what Mimi's products were? Time would tell.

This bit about running a retail store jacked Andie's stress level to the max. If Sam went to Rosemont, and that wasn't a done deal, how could she run Sam back and forth across the bay to Tampa three days a week and still help in Mimi's shop? And where did practicing magic fit in?

Nowhere! Who wanted to practice the craft, anyway? Not her. And what happened when a customer wanted to know more about one of the potions? Like Andie would know the answer?

Shopping with Sam at the Rite-Buy grocery store proved worse than negotiating a peace agreement between warring countries. Once they'd filled the cart with what Mimi wanted, Andie indulged Sam for a few things. But bargaining with him over what he liked and what she wouldn't let him have was like being with an octopus. He traded back two small packages of salty chips for one large bag, an eight-pack of dry cereal for one box of Choco-Marsho-Crunches.

This went on throughout the store. For every two things Sam put in the cart, she returned one. Aware this was his ploy, her job was to figure out which one of the two he wanted. She drew the line at four cartons of ice cream. He got one.

Heading for the cash register, she spied the loaf of white bread trapped between her peach yogurt and the container of Captain Soapy Suds shampoo. Andie stopped to extricate the loaf before it smashed into a pancake.

Sam must have seen it too. He lifted his finger. Was he planning to raise groceries in the middle of Rite-Buy? "Pinkie promise," she whispered. With a devious smile, he lowered his finger.

The gum-smacking teenage checker swept her stare over Andie and Sam, up one side and down the other. Andie pretended she didn't notice, though she was sure the cashier had overheard.

If going through the grocery store with Sam was challenging, what would a conversation about Rosemont be like? Her worry basket was so full now she didn't know where to start.

Once they were back and the groceries unloaded, Andie sat at the breakfast bar staring out to the deck. Sam tapped her arm and gestured to the tub of ice cream still on the counter.

"Oh. Honey, can you put it away for me? You can have some after dinner." He hopped down, but she stopped him before he could finish his chore. "You know what? We should have some right now. We might forget later. What do you think?"

"A good plan," Mimi said as she came into the kitchen. "Sam, make those three spoons."

"Make that four," Rhea said as she followed behind her mother.

"Let's do this the easy way," Mimi said as she popped the top off the ice cream. "Everybody dig in."

Oh, why not? If, as Mimi said, the necklace would rock her life, Andie needed all the fortification she could get.

Chapter Ten

"Table for three?" the Dockside hostess confirmed.

"Yes, three," Andie said.

Andie had finally made a dinner reservation at Brett's restaurant, putting it off partly because eating out with Sam could be tricky. Having Mimi with them would help.

Andie glimpsed Brett, waving them toward the outdoor dining area.

The other reason for her hesitation was that it meant seeing Brett again. She'd kept busy with Sam's home school lessons, supervising his play on the beach, and fretting about their future.

Those kept her mind off Brett and her on the beach. Or when he took them out to Lemon Key. She thought about him sporadically—only every few hours.

Andie, Mimi, and Sam edged through the crowd where Brett stood next to a corner table by the water. His Hawaiian shirt contrasted the torso-hugging clothes he'd worn before. Still, it fit the image of a laid-back tropical eatery.

She caught the slight hint of his spicy aftershave as Brett held the chair out for her. When Sam proudly copied him and scooted Mimi's chair out, Andie's heart swelled with pride. Earlier, she'd told Sam about the upcoming visit with his father. Since then, he'd seemed calmer and more focused. No sense pushing her luck by talking about Rosemont.

"A dolphin pod swam past just before you got here. They'll come back in a few minutes. Can I start your drinks?" Brett asked.

"White wine for me," Mimi said.

"Sam, we stock a fine brand of chocolate milk here," Brett said in a formal maître d's voice. "Would you be interested in a glass?"

Sam nodded.

Brett turned to Andie. "And for you, miss?"

"The same," she said.

"You got it." Brett strolled through the maze of diners and disappeared inside.

Sam angled a stare at his mother.

"Hey, this is a party. Chocolate milk will be perfect," she said.

At that moment, Mimi called out: "Sam, they're back."

Sam stood and tracked the dolphins with a finger. Andie sat straight up in her chair. "Don't you dare" Couldn't they have one moment's peace today without the magic rearing its dragon head?

He continued tracing their outlines as the dolphin pod glided past.

Collective oohs and awes erupted across the restaurant as one dolphin rose from the water, displayed his underbelly, and swam backward.

Andie's gut cartwheeled. "Samuel Elliott McCraig, you put that dolphin right back down."

Sam gave his mother a soulful stare and slumped into his chair.

Mimi shook her head as a "calm down" message to Andie.

"So, you saw Scorpio. This was your lucky day."

Andie's elbow slid off the table as she realized Brett stood over her shoulder.

He placed Mimi's wine and the two glasses of milk on the table. "Scorpio's a juvenile dolphin. He rarely does that back walk."

Andie rubbed her funny bone and shot a "sorry, honey" look to her son.

"Fresh grouper special today," Brett said.

Either the man was gracious or didn't hear her call out to Sam. Andie took a sip of the sweet milk and hoped for the latter.

"Grilled grouper sounds great. And a baked potato with the works," Mimi said.

"Same for me," Andie said.

Sam returned to the rail, on the lookout for more dolphins.

"Sam will have a hamburger," Andie said.

Brett gave her an odd smile and opened his mouth to say something. When he didn't and walked toward the kitchen, Andie couldn't help but wonder what that meant.

Andie snapped to attention as a tall, well-endowed woman with black pigtails stood at their table. Around Andie's age, the woman was dressed in shorts and a tight T-shirt emblazoned with the restaurant logo. She wore knee-high black stockings printed with white skeletons and Doc Martens ankle boots on her feet.

Andie glanced down at her shorts and a plain T-shirt. A place inside Andie pinged with envy at the daring and confident woman.

"Hello, there. I'm Sabrina. Brett asked me to take this table."

"Oh, hello." Andie hoped staring at Brett hadn't been too obvious.

"Let me know if you need anything else. Your dinners should be out soon." With a bemused frown, Sabrina hesitated as though she too wanted to say something more. Then, she moved on to another table.

"Should I tell her?" Mimi asked Sam.

He smiled.

"Dear, you have a milk mustache," Mimi said as she and Sam shared a giggle.

"Oh!" Andie dipped her chin as she dabbed a napkin on her mouth. No wonder Brett, Sabrina, and possibly everyone else looked at her like she was a fool. "Why didn't somebody tell me?"

Sam cocked a shoulder and smirked. Draio or not, this boy knew how to tap-dance on her last nerve. A pelican glided across the waterway and landed on the seawall below, preened its feathers, and crouched into sleep. An intelligent bird to lay low. Sam was in a mood, and no telling what he'd do next.

Brett returned to the table after they finished their meal and faced them, straddled on a backward chair. "There's time to make it across the street to the beach for sunset. Sam, have you ever seen the green flash?"

Sam's eyebrows knit together like an older man's. He shook his head.

"Well, let's do it!" Brett said.

Across the street in the still-warm sand, Brett went down on his knees beside Sam. "The Tocobagas lived all around here a long time ago and thought a green flash today meant good fishing luck tomorrow. Pay attention when I say to," he said.

Andie cast Brett a skeptical eye and shook her head. What a story. Cute, but a total fabrication that she'd never heard before. And good luck convincing this boy. Sam was savvy for his age. She knelt on Sam's other side and snapped a picture of her son and Brett as they stared at nothing more than an invented fable.

"Ready?" Brett asked. "Here we go. Look away. Look back. Blink. There. See it?"

Sam yanked on Andie's blouse to get her attention. His broad smile meant he saw something.

The whole time Andie lived here with her grandmother, never once had she seen anything close to a green flash, and tonight was no exception. That didn't stop her from admiring how these two guys bonded even though it was over an optical illusion.

It didn't matter if green flashes were real. What mattered was that Sam McCraig made his first friend in his new town. And, it seemed, so had she.

At home, Andie decided to conduct the reading lesson she owed Sam by asking him to draw pictures of the green flash.

A few quiet minutes later, he held up one to show her.

"This is excellent and going into our storybook," she said.

Andie hoped one day Sam would read his stories aloud. She was content with his written descriptions until then.

But the way he slammed his markers into the box meant he was at the far end of his attention span.

"Let's go outside and look at the stars," she said.

As Andie described the different constellations, her attention was drawn to the sound of drums in the distance. From his puzzled look, she assumed Sam heard them, too. Of course. It was a Saturday night, and this was the Baga Beach drum circle.

"You up for another adventure?" she asked.

He perked up.

"Scoot inside and get your shoes. And don't get sidetracked."

CHAPTER ELEVEN

Sam came back downstairs with Rhea. Andie hesitated to include her but decided it was the polite thing to do.

"It's drum circle night. Join us?" she asked.

"Absolutely!" Barefoot Rhea held Sam's hand, and the pair were off.

As Andie jogged to catch up, she clasped the amethyst pendant bouncing on her chest. There were only three in existence, and one was around the neck of the free spirit holding her son's hand.

The full moon's reflection on the water guided them along the soft, cool sand. Up ahead, a crowd surrounded a bonfire.

"Help me keep an eye on Sam. This is his first drum circle," Andie said.

"You worry too much," Rhea said. "He'll be fine."

But as soon as they reached the circle, Rhea released Sam's hand and began dancing her way to the center. Circles tended to go late, so it might be the last they'd see of her tonight unless she met up with some new love of her life and took off again. Andie didn't buy the idea that her mother was done being a vagabond.

What a fine shopkeeper she was going to be.

In the circle, Rhea fit right in. Young, old, and in-between were dressed in shorts and T-shirts, bathing suits, or bohemian like her mother. Some were attired in African robes or billowing skirts. Hairstyles ran the gamut from Rasta to Boho to Wall Street.

Several swirled illuminated hoops. Little children chased giant soap bubbles.

Swaying gently to the rhythm, Andie stood behind Sam and leaned down. "You okay? We can leave if you want."

He shook his head and pulled her farther toward the drummers. The tribal beat drove straight through Andie. Drums. Cowbells. Rattles and shakers. Loud enough to banish any negative thoughts. All of it was wonderful.

After a frantic upsurge in the beat, the drumming stopped, followed by an explosion of cheers and whistles.

She bent down and spoke in Sam's ear. "You still okay?"

He nodded even deeper this time as he watched his grandmother. Rhea was spinning and hip-swiveling like she'd done this a thousand times. Which she likely had.

"Andie?" someone behind her yelled. Though it sounded like Brett, what would he be doing here? He didn't seem the drum-circle type. But how would she know that?

Brett sidled up to them. "I want to introduce someone."

They trailed behind as he walked through the crowd, stopping every few feet while he greeted or hugged someone. Eventually, they stopped in front of a tall, elegant brown-skinned man dressed in a full-length African robe standing amidst an array of wooden drums.

"Hey, Brett-man," he said.

Brett and the man hugged like old friends. "Andie and Sam, meet Derrick, the best djembe player in the Bay area."

"So kind of you. You are welcome to play any of these," Derrick said.

"You game?" Brett asked.

"Absolutely," Andie said as she lowered to her knees. "Sam, pick out a drum to play."

Sam chose one that came up to his tummy and allowed him to stand next to Derrick. Sam echoed Derrick's cadence, beat for beat. Drummers, along with others playing assorted noisemakers, joined in until the collective sound rose to the sky. Sam acted like he'd been a part of this culture all his life. He was gifted in so many ways. All he needed was guidance. But from who?

Brett squatted beside her and leaned close to be heard. "I'm glad you and Sam joined us tonight." His warm breath on her neck triggered unanticipated arousal that caused her to shift off-balance and plop onto the ground. She adjusted to a cross-legged position as though she planned to sit here.

As Brett placed a drum in her lap, his hands lightly brushed her bare thighs, inches from her most private part. Instinctively she clamped her legs tight around the drum, grateful it was dark and nobody could see her red face.

Although Andie had been to drum circles before, she'd never played in one. She gave the drum a light tap, glad the surrounding drummers drowned the puny sound. Banging on a drum might discharge some of the electricity caused by Brett's touch.

An older woman in a lawn chair next to Andie leaned toward her. "Don't be afraid of it. Give it a good whack. The drum won't mind."

The woman's crackly voice startled Andie, who slammed the drumhead, causing her hands to rebound toward her chin. She scrambled to her knees and shot a look around to see if anyone noticed how stupid she must look. Tentatively, she tapped the drum again, sending a ripple of energy up her arms to a place deep in her chest, evoking something primal.

Derrick played a cadence and beckoned for her to repeat it. Andie played it back. Then he shut his eyes and disappeared into the rhythm. Others were in the same meditative trance, even the old woman in the lawn chair.

The longer Andie played, she too entered that sacred space. Time and place disappeared. Only the rhythm remained. More confident, she hit the drum hard. Then harder. Suddenly, something bubbled from inside.

Anger.

At Steven for destroying their family.

At herself for marrying the man.

She pounded until her fingers stung. And until a warm hand touched her arm.

She opened her eyes and looked up at Brett.

Everyone else had stopped drumming and applauded her. "Uh-oh."

Brett laughed. "You were great."

Andie averted her gaze and circled her palms over the drum's taut head, wishing somebody would start playing and get the attention off her. Still sitting in the sand, she slid her glance up to Brett standing beside her. He'd taken off his Hawaiian shirt and was in the process of peeling off the sweat-soaked T-shirt. Did the man have any idea how hot he looked? Every woman around stared at him—even the lawn chair lady.

Andie wiped her hand across her damp forehead. Was it the fire pit that caused the heat to rise? Or something else?

Somehow, her mother had appropriated a bundle of lit sage and walked through the crowd, waving a feather over the plume of white smoke. She circled Sam and Andie with the fragrant smoke, making an extra pass over Sam. Then Rhea saged Brett.

As the next cadence started, Brett strapped his drum over his shoulders. The djembe seductively rode his thigh as he played. Sweat beads ran down his chest and into his waistband. Andie licked her dry lips, surprised at the stirrings she thought lay buried.

It had been a long time since she'd allowed herself to experience desire. What was she supposed to do with these feelings? Should she enjoy them? Or stuff them down?

Another piercing scream came from one of three women dressed in bejeweled costumes, standing tall with her arms held high, snapping finger thimbles in time with the drums. With choreographed precision, the women began a sensual belly dance. The new drum cadence intensified, and the barefoot sirens swayed faster with impeccable moves. And right in the middle of all this? Her mother.

Thank goodness Sam was mesmerized by his drum and not the X-rated dancers. Still, Andie kept an eye on the little man. She couldn't wait to see his drawings after tonight.

One of the women looked familiar, but Andie couldn't tell for sure. The dark-haired dancer's gold-sequined bra pushed up her generous breasts. Her bare midriff dissolved into a purple chiffon skirt. She undulated with incredible flexibility until she was right in front of Brett.

The dancer's eyes homed on him as she twirled and gyrated. Her final backbend exposed a belly button ring surrounded by a rose vine tattoo that disappeared below her waistband.

Andie gripped the edge of her drum and clenched her teeth.

Why should she care about a woman dancing the seven veils in front of Brett Austin? Andie had no claim on the man. There must be a stable of women chasing him as good-looking as Brett was.

The frenzied drumbeats fell silent, though the sound echoed in Andie's ears. The dark-haired dancer rose, spun, and released another long, warbling, high-pitched wail. Then she placed a light kiss on Brett's cheek.

The woman knelt in front of Andie. "Hi. Remember me?"

All Andie could focus on was the woman's generous, heaving flesh peeking out above her bra.

"I was your server at the Dockside tonight."

Sabrina? Andie sat erect. "Well, you are certainly ... I mean, you are an amazing dancer." *And skillful seductress.*

"Thanks. Join us," Sabrina said.

The other dancers added their encouragement. "Come on." "It's easy."

The woman in the lawn chair added, "It's good for the soul."

"Then you join us, too." Sabrina extended one hand to the woman and her other to Andie.

Andie stood and slid her gaze to Brett, who waved her toward the dancers. The roaring bonfire radiated blazing heat. Why else would she feel like a boiled beet?

Sam tugged on Andie's hand. Did he want her to dance, too? Or was he about to raise something again?

A log tumbled into the fire pit and showered the air with embers. Was this what Joan of Arc saw right before her end?

Andie wasn't getting out of this, so she might as well give it a shot. She kicked off her flip-flops as the cadence began again. As Sabrina led the women into the circle, Rhea disappeared into her trance dance. If Andie could hide among the others, she might blend in.

Yeah. Like a Dalmatian in a cat show.

The Lawn-chair woman jutted her hip toward Andie. "Don't just stand there, sweetie. Move it."

Humiliation jockeyed with Andie's urge to vomit as her bare toes curled into the sand. She looked for an escape route, but she'd have to push through the four-deep circle. In the glow, they resembled zombies.

What in the world was wrong with her? Before she married Steven, she sang and played guitar at beach parties or friends' homes. Performing was performing. So how much worse could this be?

A lot worse. This had the makings of an imminent disaster served on a half-shell. And those zombies around the circle were primed to make a meal out of her brain.

Sabrina offered an enigmatic smile and danced in a circle around Andie. Oh, how insane. It's a dance. Not an execution. *Just do this.* She struck a half-spirited pose and lifted her arms à la Sabrina.

Sabrina wailed again, nearly piercing Andie's eardrum. Why did that woman keep doing that?

Andie eased into a gentle hip glide, trying her best to imitate the other women by gyrating and flicking her wrists. The drums got louder. And faster. And louder still. Until there were no sounds in the world other than drumbeats.

She couldn't get this dance at all. Maybe a good old country line dance might work with a few modifications. She tapped her toe, looking for the beat.

Thumbs in her shorts pockets, she grapevined around the crackling fire, then around a second time. When nobody threw rocks at her, Andie realized the line dance worked. That old lady was happy, too.

The wispy sage smoke and the drumbeats were intoxicating. Sand cupped her steps as she followed the sound of the tinkling bells on Sabrina's belt.

No longer Andie Tanner McCraig, she had entered a lovely place where her cares had dissipated. Was this what finding herself was like? If so, she loved every bit of it.

Then the drumming abruptly stopped. Sabrina's high-pitched warble rose to the sky and yanked Andie back to earth. Her eyes snapped open. She froze in place, eye-to-eye with Brett. Scorched by the intensity in his eyes and breathless from the dance, her heart rate skyrocketed.

She managed a weak smile. Though she wanted to wipe away the perspiration coursing between her breasts, it would have to go it alone. She wasn't about to draw attention to her chest.

The drumming started again, but Andie could barely hear it. Brett's dark eyes sparkled in the firelight, and his unwavering gaze drove deep into her core. Could he see the loneliness there? Would he be the one to take that away?

Then from the corner of her eye, she spotted Sam holding up his bobbing head. Poor kid.

"I need to get my guy to bed," she said as she backed away. "This was fun, Brett. I'm glad you talked me into staying."

Brett put his drum back with Derrick's others, stuffed his t-shirt in his shorts' back waistband, and put on the Hawaiian shirt. "I'll walk with you."

"We'll be fine." She didn't trust herself around Brett any longer tonight.

She tickled Sam's ear. "Come on, honey. Time to go."

Sam looked up, his eyes barely open, then reached to her.

Drums and dancing had taken it out of her. "Honey, you're too heavy to carry."

"Up you go." Brett lifted Sam and adjusted his hold on him. "Austin Rideshare at your service."

The Lawn-chair lady sidled up and crooked her finger for Andie to bend down.

"Dearie, if you ever get bored with that beautiful man of yours, just let me know, and I'll come-a running! He's delicious."

Andie giggled. "He's not 'my man.'"

"The heck he ain't. I've been watching you two all night. Nope. You both got it bad."

Chapter Twelve

After carrying Sam upstairs, Brett should have gone home, except Andie had insisted he stay awhile.

He came back downstairs while Andie put Sam to bed.

Andie had truly enjoyed herself tonight. It showed in the drumming, her dancing, and on her gorgeous face. Mimi would have been proud.

She deserved someone who could make her happy like this all the time.

Andie came down the stairs. "Sam's dead to the world." She opened the wine cabinet. "Can I offer you something? As you can see, Mimi has a well-stocked selection."

He had no good reason to leave other than tempting fate by staying.

"Allow me." Brett opened a cabernet, poured two glasses, and brought them to the kitchen island.

"Cheers." Brett tipped his glass to Andie's. He took a sip and inspected the stack of Sam's drawings lying on the counter. "Sam's a musician and a talented artist."

"The musician part was news to me." Andie's phone chimed. "It's Jason."

Brett finished his wine. "I should be going."

Andie waved him to stay, then put the phone on speaker. "Jason, Brett's here with me. When do you get in?"

"Tomorrow."

"Where are you flying in from, man?" Brett asked.

"Boston."

"Dude, bring me some *lobstah* rolls," Brett said mirthfully, earning Andie's smile.

"You got it, bro. I expect grouper in return," Jason said.

Someone tapped on the slider.

"Rhea's home," Andie announced and went to the door to unlock it.

"Wasn't that a great circle? I could dance all night. Except I'm exhausted." Rhea primped her hair and tucked in a stray dreadlock. She made a sweeping, barefooted swirl around the kitchen, then sat on a stool next to Brett. "I'm not as young as I look."

"Mother?" Jason's disembodied voice came from the phone lying on the counter.

"My love! Where are you?" Rhea iced each word with glee.

"Boston. I'll be there tomorrow," Jason said.

"How exciting to have both my babies here," Rhea said.

Andie ducked her head and huffed a laugh.

After the call, Rhea went upstairs to bed.

"One more?" Brett asked?

"Sure. I'm not driving." Her sweet little sexy smile was unnerving.

Brett carefully refilled his and Andie's glasses.

"Watching Sam enjoy himself makes it harder to decide what I'm going to do." She picked out a bit of cork that floated on the surface of her wine.

Brett thought the woman had guts even to try tackling Sam's magic alone. He looked through the boy's drawings again.

"These are good," he said.

"It's almost scary how he picks up the tiniest details. His speech therapist explained that it's his compensating mechanism for not verbally describing things. Look at how he draws the eyes."

Brett turned to a picture that was undeniably Andie. Sam had nailed it. But sad was the only word to describe her.

Andie laughed. "Of course, you would pick that one."

Brett shut the sketchbook and looked up at her. "That's much better. Sam needs to draw a new one with you smiling like you are now."

She ducked her head, and the smile disappeared. Why? What had he said? Obviously, the wrong thing.

After a night of drumming and two glasses of wine, he'd better leave before he made it worse.

"You need some rest. Now's not the time to make decisions," Brett said.

If she were any other woman and not Jason's sister, he'd take her in his arms. But Andie was vulnerable. He didn't want to confuse her by sending the wrong message.

After they walked to the front door, she stood temptingly near as he reached for the doorknob. Why didn't she step back? He shifted away, but she still blocked his exit.

"Andie, I need to leave." He reached for her arms to ease her aside. She didn't budge. Didn't she understand how hard it was for him to resist her? His hand grazed her neck and brushed the soft skin on her jaw.

Time collapsed somewhere between any well-meaning thoughts when his lips found hers. Warm. Eager. Gentle. Demanding. Tasting of wine.

His hands circled her back. After a night of dancing, the heady mix of her scent joined with his. She was delicious.

ANDIE PUSHED BACK, her lips swollen from the whirling kaleidoscope of their kiss. She glanced over Brett's shoulder to the stairs.

"Sam?" She forgot the world while in Brett's arms. Even her son.

"Busted." Brett's nervous laugh poured over her like ice water.

She fought a wave of nausea. How would she explain this to Sam? Or to herself?

Adrenaline fueled her sprint upstairs behind Sam, whose feet hammered each step. If only the boy had made this much noise coming down. A small gust blew against her as their shared bedroom door slammed. Only once before had he shut her out—the time he heard her and Steven in a bitter argument.

A deep breath failed to tame the wild horses bucking her insides. She opened the door. In the darkness, moonlight through the window exposed a lump in the middle of Sam's bed. His sheet, drawn over his head, barely muffled his sobs.

She sent a quick prayer skyward, asking to make this right by him.

"Sam, I know you're in there." Andie sat on the edge of the bed. "I'm not going away, so you might as well come out."

He kicked the sheets. Sam was smart as a professor. Cute as a puppy. Stubborn as a mule.

She flipped on the lamp beside his bed. "Fine. Be that way. But it's going to get hot under there."

Sam threw back the sheet and glowered at her.

"Sometimes kisses happen. Grownups do silly things." *Very silly.* "Are you worried I would go away?"

Sam shook his head.

"You know your daddy and I are not married anymore, right?"

He shifted his glance away from her.

"Someday, your daddy or I, or both of us, will have a new person in our lives. But never think that means I don't love you. You are the best thing that ever happened to me."

Sam seemed to consider this a long moment.

"Want me to stay with you a while?" she asked.

He shook his head again.

She kissed his forehead. "I love you, Sam. More than cupcakes."

After she tucked him in and left the bedroom, she stood a few moments at the top of the stairs. From here, she could see Brett on the sofa, sitting forward, arms across his thighs, and his head hung low.

Before their kiss, she'd had a choice and, once again, impulsively picked wrong. Brett's warm touch reminded her how wonderful a man's embrace could be. But the look of betrayal in Sam's eyes erased all those selfish thoughts.

That brief moment had changed the rules. Andie had to be sure Brett knew that.

Somehow.

BRETT SQUEEZED his fingers until his knuckles popped. He'd taken advantage of Andie in a weak moment. Wasn't he a better man than that?

"He'll be fine," she assured him.

Brett's heart skipped a beat at the sound of her voice.

"This," she said quietly. "I mean the kiss. Shouldn't have..." She turned her gaze upstairs. "There can't be anything like that between us."

Her message was loud and clear. And she was right. "The more we talk about it, the worse we'll make it," he said.

Her glistening eyes made him think she had more to say. But like him, she couldn't find the words.

All he could manage was, "Don't forget to lock up."

Chapter Thirteen

"Fine, then. Keep Sam a prisoner in this house for the rest of his life. That's a good solution." Mimi stood in Andie's bedroom doorway, watching her fold laundry. "And every time he lifts a finger, you'll have a cow that he will destroy something."

Andie and her grandmother had been sparring over Rosemont Academy since breakfast. She couldn't tell if Mimi was deliberately agitating a decision out of her or if her grandmother was honestly at her wits' end.

Whichever one it was, Andie didn't need this right now. Kissing Brett last night had derailed Andie's rational thoughts, and right now, she needed to be at the top of her game. She hoped she'd made it clear to Brett that she wasn't interested in a relationship.

Although she and Steven had fallen out of love long before he left, when she told Sam that grownups sometimes do silly things, deep down, she didn't feel kissing Brett was silly at all.

Andie's focus came back to the present moment and her grandmother still extolling the virtues of Rosemont Academy.

After putting the last of the laundry away, Andie slammed the dresser drawer. "Mimi, I can help Sam just as well as strangers can. I will not ship him off to some school for wizards."

"What can I do to convince you? I swear you are the stubbornest person in this family." Mimi's words dripped with exasperation as she followed Andie downstairs.

"Worse than me?" Rhea, Alika in her lap, watched cartoons beside Sam.

"Apples don't fall far from the tree," Mimi said.

That old chestnut didn't help Andie one bit. "Mimi, Sam's sitting right in front of you."

"Pffft." Mimi rolled her eyes. "I'll bet he has some of both of you in him."

Andie's phone buzzed with a call from Jason. "Where are you?" she asked.

"At the front door. I've been knocking and ringing the bell. You throwing a party in there?"

"Sam," Andie called out. "Turn the TV down and get the door. It's your Uncle Jason. And open it the normal way, please."

"Jason, my love!" Rhea dumped the cat off her lap and spun in pirouettes toward the door.

Mimi and Andie looked at each other and shook their heads.

"Why can't we be like normal humans and calmly greet each other less theatrically?" Andie asked.

Mimi squeezed Andie's hand. "You realize there's not a single normal human in this family."

Jason Tanner, at six foot six, barely cleared the doorframe. He left his bags and airline Captain's hat by the stairs, then hoisted Sam. The boy clamped his legs around his uncle's waist. Towering over Rhea, Jason used his free arm to hug his mother.

He eased Sam down and hugged Mimi, then turned to Andie. She fought back joyful tears to have an ally.

"Don't start that." Jason's strong hug lifted his sister three inches off the floor.

"Thank goodness you're here," Andie said.

He gently released her back down. "Missed you, kid."

"All my babies are here," Rhea said, clapping her hands.

Andie scanned the motley cast of characters. Her son dashed around the room, playing with the model airplane Jason had given him and wearing his uncle's hat, two times too big for him.

Jason, in his starched white shirt and blue slacks. Rhea a stark contrast to any of them. Mimi enthroned on a barstool like a matriarchal grande dame.

And herself relieved Sam didn't fly the plane via his Draio remote control.

Mimi was so right. Not a single one of them was anywhere near normal.

"This calls for a glass of my special honey mead!" Mimi announced. "I'll be right back."

"And I need a shower." Jason grabbed his bag and followed Mimi upstairs.

"Let's celebrate on the deck," Rhea said as she went on outside.

"I'll get the glasses," Andie said.

"You would be wise to listen to your grandmother," Alika said.

Andie's heart jumped to her throat as she fumbled with the glasses she saved from shattering on the granite counter. She shifted her stare to the floor as the black cat came into focus through a watery cloud.

Alika sat in front of her. "My humble apologies. My entrances are quite unsophisticated."

Andie's shoulders slumped. "I thought you went outside with Rhea."

"I needed a word with you."

"Oh, is that right?" *This cat was certainly full of himself.*

"I heard that."

"Thought you turned that off?"

The cat shrugged. "I forgot. Listen to me as I will not say this twice."

"Don't feel compelled to say it," Andie said.

"I'll ignore that. Now then. Your young man is quite an exceptional child. He will need the finest mentoring. You seem like a nice lady, but I am not certain you have the qualifications for this assignment."

"Well, aren't you the little knowledge bucket!"

"Unlike your other comments, I will accept this one as a compliment since I am known for my wisdom."

"Not when it comes to my family business. Sam is my son, and I make the decisions about his future."

"I only offer suggestions. But you would be smart to take them." Alika trotted to the closed slider and disappeared through it.

"What's with that freaking feline?" Andie growled under her breath. Perhaps she was stubborn, but that cat was downright arrogant.

Mimi returned with a quart of amber-colored liquid. "This has been in my apothecary for two years. High time we enjoyed it. I see your mother's already installed outside."

Jason, who'd showered and changed in record time, joined them. He performed the honors and uncorked the bottle. A more potent drink than Andie preferred, mead seemed suitable for the occasion.

"Is that the doorbell?" Andie gripped her brother's arm.

"Hey! Watch it. Those nails of yours are lethal." Jason rubbed four red marks on his forearm.

She ignored him and checked the time. It was after eight. Who was it? They weren't expecting any deliveries.

"Wait! Don't open it." Andie looked around for Sam, safe outside in Mimi's lap.

"Take it easy. You expecting the boogie man?" Jason asked as he went to the door.

Andie wouldn't be surprised if it were Steven. So, same as.

"Go on outside," Jason said. "We'll be right out."

Who's this "we?" She waited inside, arms folded over her chest while Jason opened the door.

"Appreciate the text," Brett said as he gave Jason a man-hug.

"Hope you're okay that I invited him," Jason said.

Brett glanced at Andie, but she averted his gaze. Jason had every right to invite his friends over. And that's what this was—a gathering of friends.

Andie went ahead of them out to the deck.

"Mother, how's the mead?" Jason asked.

"We're about to find out." Rhea half-filled everyone's glasses with the honey blend.

"Wait! Before we drink, I need to make the Tanner toast," Mimi said.

"To all assembled here,

We raise a glass of cheer.

May our bonds be strong,

As here we belong.

Together there is no one to fear!"

After they all tapped their glasses, Andie took a sip of the amber concoction. It had been years since she'd had homemade mead. The sweet, fruity elixir reminded her of how the eldest Tanner, usually her grandfather, would open a bottle or two. No family celebration ever started without the toast and the drink.

She shut her eyes and enjoyed how a slight hint of bubbles tickled the roof of her mouth. She swallowed slowly to enjoy the warmth as the liquid coursed down her throat. When she opened her eyes, Brett's gaze riveted on her as he tipped his glass toward her. His broad smile sent another spiral of warmth through her.

"More?" Rhea said as she came around to each of them.

Did she mean more of Brett or the mead?

"Just a drop," Andie said.

Rhea poured much more than a drop, but Andie paced herself. She wouldn't overindulge and make a total fool of herself.

Sam tugged at Andie's shirt and pointed to her glass.

"It's the custom to take a sniff first," Andie said.

He stuck his nose into the glass, scowled, and pulled back. Precisely the reaction she'd hoped he'd have.

"I have an idea," Mimi said. "There's more ice cream in the freezer. And I think there's chocolate syrup in the cupboard. Would you like some if it's all right with your mother?"

Before Andie could answer, Sam was inside and on the kitchen stool.

"So, Mother. Have you thought about what you want your grandkids to call you?" Jason asked.

In lotus position on one of the chaise lounges, Rhea answered: "Are you trying to tell me something, Jason?"

"No, Mother. It's just a question," he answered.

"Well, you know I'm just an old-fashioned girl." As she tucked a stray dreadlock behind her ear, one of her dozen bracelets caught in her hair. "Dammit!"

Once she shimmied it free, she finished her mead in one long gulp. "I want them to call me Grandma."

Andie exchanged a bemused glance with Jason as they simultaneously mouthed, *Grandma?* But if Sam could talk, she wouldn't care what he called Rhea.

"I'm going up to my room. It's past time for my nightly meditation." Rhea held her palms together and bowed. "Namaste."

"So you know, Jason, nothing's changed," Andie said once Rhea had gone inside. "And her familiar could be anywhere around here. Anything you say or think is fair game for it."

"The black cat? I saw it trail behind her up the stairs," Jason said.

"You saw it?" Andie's anger interlaced with surprise.

"If it matters, I did too. It was beside your mother all evening," Brett said.

Of course, they could see it. They were both Draio, like her son.

"I think the thing hates me," Andie said.

The guys had launched into their conversation and ignored her comment. But this gave her a chance to watch them together. It seemed like yesterday that they were school pals. Little League. Boogie-boarding. Playing with their Game Boys. Basketball in Mimi's driveway.

And Brett yanking her hair.

Jason poured the rest of his mead over the deck rail. "Too sweet for me. I'll get us some beer. Mimi always stocks the garage fridge."

Andie had known Brett since elementary school, but being alone with him was awkward after that kiss. A curious tugging in her heart reminded her that he wasn't a boy any longer, and she wasn't just Jason's kid sister.

If only she hadn't been so dead set on marrying Steven. If only she hadn't bought into the man's promises. If only things had been different, would she and Brett have been a couple?

If. Always an *if.*

The reality was she had married, moved away, and had a son.

Getting her and Sam's life on track was the number one reason she was home. Not sitting here mooning over Brett like a high-school kid.

"Thank you again for dinner last night," she said, skating around the elephant between them.

"Not a problem. What'd you think of Sabrina?"

Sabrina? Why ask about her? "Well, she's nice. A good dancer, too."

"Yeah. I don't know what I'd do without her. I asked her to—"

Before he finished the sentence, Jason returned with the beer. The guys popped theirs open while Andie set hers on the table, glad for the darkness that hid her embarrassment. Brett was about to tell her he'd asked Sabrina to marry him. And oddly, she didn't want to hear him say it. And what a jerk! His kiss had more passion than an X-rated movie, and he was going to marry somebody else?

"It's Sam's bath and bedtime. I hope you two will keep it down." Andie raced into the house.

BRETT KEPT his gaze fixed in the direction of the kitchen, keeping quiet until Andie had escorted Sam upstairs. What had he done to spook her? He had tried to keep the conversation light while she was with them.

"What's your take?" he asked.

"I'm sensing something's coming," Jason said. "That's really why I'm here."

Had he been communing with Sabrina?

"One of my staff is prescient and saw something, too," Brett said.

"A Draio, also? Poor guy," Jason said.

Brett laughed. "It's a woman. But she had a vision about a boy before she even knew Sam was here. She couldn't get a clear picture."

"Same here. I think it's something to do with that asshat Steven."

Brett crushed his empty beer can with one hand. "Doesn't surprise me. She hasn't made up her mind about how to mentor Sam yet. Mimi's been on her case to unite the power of three."

"With my mother as part of that?" Jason rolled his eyes. "With my schedule, I wouldn't be any help." Jason finished his beer and opened another that he offered to Brett. "You know, you would be a great mentor for him."

Brett let out a long breath. "You know why not."

"You got a better idea?"

"Rosemont," Brett said.

Jason shook his head. "There has to be another option."

Not enough beer or honey mead on the planet could help Brett come up with a better suggestion. A deep place inside told him to ride like an avenging knight, sword raised high, and blaze his way into Andie's life to save the day. Except with his luck, he'd fall face-first off the horse.

His head warned him to stay uninvolved and detached. His heart told him that the beautiful Andie, upstairs getting her little boy ready for bed, needed help.

Somehow this help would have to be from him. Right now, he had no idea how.

Chapter Fourteen

Two men and a boy. An excellent name for a headbanger band. Instead, this fit Brett, Jason, and Sam standing in the ticket line at the Tampa Zoo.

Sam had been around far too many females in Mimi's house. He needed some guy-bonding time. Jason had softened Andie to the idea of him and Brett taking Sam on a field trip. But only after promising they'd keep the boy out of the lion's cage.

This was an exaggerated fear for Ordinary humans, but who knew what trouble Sam could get into? Jason had reminded her that both he and Brett were Draio, too, and they could take good care of him.

So Brett hoped.

They'd also been cautioned about giving into Sam's food cravings, or they'd deal with a sick kid. But once inside the gate, the first thing Sam spotted was a snack bar. He yanked on Jason's hand and pulled him to the menu sign, where he traced the words "ice cream."

Brett barely stifled a laugh at Jason's lame bargaining skills. "How about after lunch? ... It's only ten o'clock. ... Don't you want to see the animals first?"

Minutes later, Sam held up his cone for Brett's appreciation.

"Good choice." Brett glanced at Jason, who narrowed his gaze back. "A vanilla swirl with birthday cake sprinkles. Looks great."

Sam ate about half before the rest fell out of the cone and splattered all over his T-shirt. His lower lip trembled, and Brett felt sorry for the boy.

"Let's take a pit stop and get that off." Brett didn't want to fuel Andie's barrage of questions about what Sam ate.

The restroom only had an air dryer. "Any ideas, Sam?"

The boy slipped off his shirt and held it under the faucet. Water splashed on Sam's naked belly, the floor, and walls but not anywhere near the ice cream splotch.

Jason came in. "What's the hold-up?" He assessed the situation and stepped up to the sink, holding up the mostly dry shirt. "How is this possible?" He surveyed the water puddles on the floor.

Behind them stood an attendant with a mop. The guy forced a smile. "No worries. I'll clean it up. Once you're finished."

Brett grabbed the shirt and ran water over the spots. Eventually, they were less noticeable, though the shirt was now soaking wet. He wrung it out as best as possible, then glanced in the mirror.

"Jason," he said quietly.

"I see it."

With looks of shock, the attendant and three others stood mystified. The attendant's mop bucket was floating at least four feet up.

Even with their Draiocht, neither Jason nor Brett could lower the bucket, dangling and swaying like a stalled cable car.

"Sam, put it back down, please." Brett shifted his gaze to a boy filming on his phone.

Sam shook his head vigorously with pure joy in his eyes.

"Freeze them," Jason said in a low whisper. "Wipe their memories before anybody else comes in here. And clear the phone."

Brett raised his hands and swept them in an arc, internally calling up the ancient gift.

Except all that came to mind was a flashback. The night the punk came out of the shadows with a gun.

And how Brett had failed to freeze him. Manny had wrestled with the boy, and the gun fired. His Draiocht had failed, and Manny died.

Brett dropped his hands to his side. "I can't."

Jason tossed the wet T-shirt to Brett, where it smacked across his chest. "Then take Sam out. Now."

Brett found a "closed for cleaning" sign and put it in front of the door. He and Sam sat on a bench in a sunny spot, the shirt draped over his knees, hoping this would help it dry faster.

Eventually, Jason casually strolled out of the restroom as though the world was spinning on its right axis. Brett and Sam scooted over so Jason could sit beside them.

"They'll be none the wiser." After several minutes of silence, Jason cleared his throat while still looking straight at the restroom doorway. "This is our secret. Do you both understand?"

Brett and Sam nodded.

"Andie can never know."

Brett and Sam nodded again.

"Anybody for a burger?" Jason asked.

Sam's shirt had dried enough so he could put it on before entering the restaurant. After lunch and more of Sam's nonverbal assurances that their secret was safe, they continued their trek through the zoo. They passed the video kid, who didn't recognize them, thanks to Jason's quick Draiocht. But no thanks to Brett's failure, once again.

Brett bought a blank page notebook perfect for Sam's drawings in one of the gift shops.

Delighted, Sam gave Brett a high-five thank you.

By two o'clock, the zoo was getting crowded.

"Time for one more stop before we head home," Jason said.

Brett noticed the rhino exhibit sign. "How about here?"

The line for hand-feeding the animal was short, and soon Sam was the next.

Brett leaned down to Sam. "You got this, right? No air feeding."

Sam looked down at his feet, then stepped up to the food tray.

"Go ahead. Take some," Jason encouraged.

To Sam, the rhino must have seemed bigger than a house. As the animal nudged the wood fence, Sam stiffened.

"It just means he's hungry." Brett stood beside Sam and took a kale leaf. "Feed him like this."

The rhino opened his mouth wide enough to consume a football and gently took the kale with one bite.

"See how easy?" Brett asked. "Now you do it."

Sam grabbed several leaves and held them out. When the rhino made a snorting sound and opened his mouth, Sam jumped back and let go of the kale. The leaves floated in midair for what seemed like hours before the animal grabbed them.

Brett's eyes darted to either side. "Did anyone see that?"

Jason cleared any bystander's memories before tapping Brett's shoulder. "Come on. Time to go."

While Sam slept in the back seat of Jason's rental car, Brett spoke in a low tone. "No wonder Andie's such a watchdog."

"The bathroom stunt was for fun." Jason's jaw tightened. "The rhino one was not."

Brett pressed the bridge of his nose. "I couldn't do a damn thing to help either time." Without a doubt, he wasn't the one to help Andie.

"He has to control it and fast. There's only one other option," Jason said.

Dear God. Rosemont was in for a treat.

Andie rinsed the dishes in the sink before putting them in the dishwasher. She noticed Jason and Sam had hardly touched their dinner. "What's wrong with you two? Grace's lasagna was awesome."

Though they tried to be sneaky, she caught their shared smirk.

"Okay. You guys ate all day, didn't you?" She'd warned her brother and Brett about this.

"Just a burger and a soda for lunch," Jason said.

Sam, eyes wide as saucers, whipped his head toward his uncle. Andie couldn't miss that red flag.

"Uh-huh. And?" Andie asked.

"Ice cream." Jason quickly added, "But he didn't eat it all."

Sam giggled, and Andie decided to drop it. But she had an idea that ice cream might be a chapter in a much larger story about zoo day.

"I told Brett I'd meet him at the Dockside for a beer. I won't stay out too late," Jason said.

"You're a big boy. Stay as long as you want." Andie held her hand out. "Leave the car fob here."

"Good plan." He waved his phone at Andie on his way out. "You know how to reach me."

Andie cleaned off the bar top. "Sam, let's sit in the living room. While I watch TV, you can draw me some pictures in your new book."

Sam sprawled on the floor while she watched a rom-com movie. He'd have enough pictures at the rate he filled pages to keep their writing lessons going for a week.

She had to give her brother and Brett credit. Sam's zoo trip was a good idea, and Brett was sweet to buy Sam a new sketchbook. With Sam safe with the two guys, she'd spent the day helping prep Mimi's new shop.

The big surprise was how focused her mother had been. Rhea worked hard and long, accomplishing more than Andie could ever remember. They assembled three shelving units, cleaned the windows, hung beaded curtains, and painted the bathroom. When Andie left at 5 p.m., her mother had just started outlining the mural she wanted to paint. No doubt the woman would be there all night working on it.

Mimi came downstairs from her apothecary and joined Andie.

"I see the boys made it home in good shape," Mimi said.

Andie lowered the volume on the TV. "So far, so good. I'm fairly confident the three musketeers made pigs of themselves, though."

"Bring your sketchbook up here, Sam," Mimi said.

Sam squeezed between his mother and Mimi and turned to the first zoo page drawing. His detail was so good that Andie could distinguish the different animals. Though his spelling was a little off, each animal's name appeared under each picture.

When Sam turned a page showing nothing but a giant ice cream cone, Andie exclaimed, "Ah-ha! I knew it."

"Sprinkles are my favorite," Mimi said.

Andie swallowed a laugh. When Sam turned to the next page, she leaned forward. "That's you. But where's your shirt?"

Sam shook his head and tried to turn the page.

"Hold on." Andie put her hand on Sam's. "Let's look at that again."

Very slowly, Sam moved his hand.

"Pretty good tummy detail," Mimi said with a chuckle. "Even a belly button."

Good detail indeed. Right down to the sink and a toilet. But what was that thing hanging in the air?

"Honey, how about you write a little story about this picture," Andie said.

When Sam hesitated, Mimi added, "I'd love it if you would."

After a deep sigh, Sam chose a blue marker and started to write. He was very particular with his letters, so Andie knew to be patient. With the volume on mute, Andie switched through some stations.

When he was done, Sam handed his book to Mimi.

"Oh, this is wonderful writing. And you print so nicely." Mimi rubbed her chin and nodded approval as though the boy had written a world-class novel.

Andie beamed. "He does so well with his schoolwork. I'm proud of him."

Mimi winked at Andie. "Let me read it out loud to your mother."

"Uncle Jason gave me ice cream. Some got on my shirt." Mimi looked over at Sam, still wearing the same shirt. "Somebody did a good job getting it off."

Mimi's gaze narrowed as she looked at the following picture. "Sam, did this really happen?"

"What do you mean *really happen?*" Andie mustered self-control, dreading what she was about to hear.

Mimi cleared her throat and continued. "I made a bucket go up. It did not come down. I sat with Brett. Uncle Jason said we could not tell."

Grace's lasagna curdled in Andie's stomach.

"Sam?" she asked.

He shrugged.

"And what's this business about Jason saying you couldn't tell?" Andie fought to hold in her anger.

Sam stared at the TV.

"Let me see that book," Andie said, but Mimi snatched it first.

"Why, Sam. Your pictures are so good. I can tell Uncle Jason from Brett. Look at their big smiles. And that's a wonderful rhinoceros. Can I help you spell that word?"

"Mimi," Andie cautioned. "That isn't helping."

Andie didn't want to scare Sam, but she needed to get to the bottom of this.

"Sam, honey. That looks like a green leaf. Why is it dangling in the air?" But Andie already knew.

"Was it the wind?" Mimi asked.

Sam shook his head and tapped his chest.

No wonder Jason and Brett wore those big, sloppy smiles. Instead of watching over Sam, they'd let him run amok. Andie thought her head would explode.

"Did anyone else see this happen?" Andie asked.

Sam moved his hands over and around his head, then opened them wide to the sky. As though he was washing something away.

One of Sam's chaperone clowns must have cleared the regular humans' memories. This was precisely the drama she'd hoped to avoid. How could they have coached a little boy into displaying magic, something downright dangerous in the Ordinary community?

"Oh, my. Look at the time. It's past somebody's bedtime." Mimi stood and took Sam's hand.

Sam kissed Andie on the cheek and nearly pulled Mimi's arm from the socket as he raced up the stairs, dragging his great-grandmother with him.

Andie clutched the amethyst on the chain around her neck. "So much for pinkie promises," she whispered to herself.

Chapter Fifteen

After a fitful night, Andie came to a painful conclusion.

If Sam hung around here much longer, everyone in the household would have him performing tricks like a carnival sideshow.

She had to enroll Sam in Rosemont.

Andie slipped out of bed and headed downstairs for coffee. She had to break this news to Sam before they visited the Academy. Her half-hearted commitment to help run Mimi's store meant commuting to Tampa twice daily. If her mother, for once, would display a modicum of reliability, she could run the store.

"Morning, sis."

Andie jumped at her brother's greeting. Distracted in thought, she didn't realize someone had come into the kitchen. Looking like something pulled from the bottom of a ragbag, Jason poured a cup of coffee. He leaned against the counter, yawning and shaking off sleep. Or a hangover. She hoped it was a real skull-crusher. He deserved it after yesterday.

"How about a nice, big, greasy plate of bacon?" she asked with a smirk. "And a side of runny undercooked eggs?"

Jason scrunched his face and sat across from Andie. "Ha-ha."

"Big night?"

"We had some catching up to do."

"Right. And did it involve females?"

"Nope, believe it or not. What could I do when your host owns the bar and the drinks are on the house?"

"At least you aren't flying anywhere today, Mr. Prim and Proper."

Mimi and Rhea joined them, taking a seat on either side of Jason. They grilled him worse than she had about his night out.

Seated across from her as the three were, Andie felt like she was in front of a grand jury. All that was missing was that snooty cat.

If you're around, yes, I said you were snooty.

She waited for the feline to lecture her again. When he didn't, she decided it was time to announce her decision. If only everyone would shut up for a second.

"Can I get a word in here?" she asked loudly.

All three bristled to attention, their conversation hanging like that rhino food in Sam's drawing.

"I've given this a lot of thought. I've been here over a week, and it's not working exactly as I hoped." Andie caught their looks—from her mother's surprise and her grandmother's worried concern to her brother's still hung-over pain.

"I don't understand," Mimi said. "What did we do?"

Andie shook her head. "It's not so much what you've done or haven't done. It's about me and the decisions I need to make about my son."

"You're not going back to that jerk Steven are you?" Jason asked.

"Not in a million years. But I decided Sam should attend Rosemont. I'll get an apartment on that side of Tampa."

"But what about us working together in the store?" Rhea's eyes had welled with tears.

Mimi reached for Andie's hand. "This is a one hundred eighty degrees turn from what you'd said before. Are you sure?"

"Positive." She paused and stared at Jason until he lifted his head and made eye contact. "After yesterday."

"What about yesterday?" Jason demanded.

As though he didn't know. "I understand the zoo experience was interesting."

Jason's eyes popped wide open. "Who told you?"

Andie sported a Cheshire cat smile. "Let's say it was reported to me. Anyway, it seems Sam may never be able to forget the magic, as I'd hoped."

Her gaze scanned the motley trio. "Sam needs a consistent, disciplined environment."

Jason looked at each woman sitting beside him. "So you're telling us that you think we're not that environment?"

A moment of uncomfortable silence ended with an eruption of laughter all around.

"Well done, granddaughter. I'll arrange a visit as soon as you tell Sam," Mimi said.

"I still think you should give the power of three a chance," Rhea said.

The likelihood of that happening was about as remote as meeting little men from outer space.

"You're kidding!" Brett's shout into his phone turned the Dockside staff's heads. He dashed out the back door to the parking lot. "I didn't tell her, Jason. And if you didn't, who did?"

"Beats me," Jason said. "But she knows. And she's decided to send Sam to Rosemont."

Brett felt gut-punched. "I thought she hated that place."

"I thought so, too. And she's moving to Tampa."

Moving?

"I think we screwed up," Jason said.

Brett's heart hardened. "This has nothing to do with you."

This one was all on him and that freaking kiss.

Brett returned to the Dockside outdoor seating area and stood at the railing, staring but not seeing.

Sabrina handed Brett a cup of coffee. "You all right? You look like a cat's hairball. Anything you want to talk about?"

Brett shook his head. He didn't want to think or talk about it. Once Andie and Sam settled on the other side of the bay, they wouldn't be back.

"If you feel better later, I need your undivided attention to go over the books. I spent most of yesterday working on them," Sabrina said.

He wasn't going to feel better later or ever. How could he let Andie get under his skin like this?

She'd trusted Sam with him and Jason, and they'd boggled it. No. He'd boggled it. Some role model he was.

"Brett?"

He shook off his thoughts. "Yeah. Sure. Soon as I've had a shower. Say in an hour?"

Brett's idea of fun did not include a two-hour conversation about ledgers and balance sheets. Thank goodness Sabrina was a natural at explanations. To him, numbers might as well be hieroglyphics.

After proving the Dockside was in the black, he asked her to consider the manager position one more time.

"Sabrina, you're smart. You know this place inside and out. You read people better than anyone I know. And from what you've shown me, I could hire you at twenty-five percent more than I paid the last one."

"No, Brett," Sabrina said.

"Then thirty percent more," he said.

Sabrina shook her head. "Before I came here, I was a personal assistant and housekeeper for a fantastic woman. They paid me well. I could come and go as I pleased. After kicking around the world, I thought I'd found a home. Then, one day, the hemmed-in feeling came over me again."

"Solange Ford in Georgia gave you a glowing reference," Brett said.

He'd never told her that his father's company conducted a deep background check and not just employment history. Hiring a magical is a whole lot more complicated than hiring Ordinaries.

It turned out Sabrina was a misunderstood Draio like Brett. She had lived on the streets since she was sixteen. No criminal record but no stranger to law enforcement, either. Solange Ford was a wise woman and had known all that when she hired Sabrina. Brett knew it too.

"It's hard to explain. It just happens," Sabrina said. "When it comes over me, I'm gone. And I know that's going to happen here, too."

"Believe me, I understand. I didn't stay in one spot long before I settled back here. Look, I don't expect a lifetime, Sabrina. I'd be happy if you gave me one more year or two. Or three."

Sabrina tossed her head back and laughed out loud. "Three is a stretch. How about we take it month by month?"

"I can live with that," Brett said.

She held out her hand. "And thirty-five percent more. You're good for it."

Brett rolled his eyes as he shook her hand. "Deal."

Chapter Sixteen

Andie and Sam, with his box of markers and new sketchbook, stood in front of Rhea's mural.

No surprise, it had a retro eighties street-art feel. Bold colors and lines. Abstract shapes that might be humans—if humans had three eyes.

Rhea came from the back, wiping her hands on a towel, with Alika prancing behind her.

"What do you think?" Rhea flashed a proud smile.

Overall, it might or might not be gallery-ready. But boy, did it look like Rhea Tanner's work.

"It's interesting," Andie said, dodging as best she could. "But Sam's my resident artist. What do you think?"

Sam canted his head from side to side, then focused on one spot: images that looked like three spaceships, then glanced back at Rhea.

"Ah. Shall I tell you my inspiration for those?" Rhea asked.

Andie bit her lower lip. What crazy story were they about to hear?

"For a long time, I've been fascinated with outer space." She stood a moment quietly, then continued. "I'm convinced there's another life form out there. We can't be alone. Sometimes, in my meditation, I see those ships, Sam. Especially the big one. Just like I painted."

Sam made a long, slow head nod as though he seriously considered what she'd said. Or, like Andie, was he convinced Rhea was a few degrees off from true north?

"You two stay as long as you want. I promised mother I'd help her box up inventory so we can start setting up this week." Rhea made another of her signature pirouettes in the middle of the shop. "Come, Alika. We're off."

Off, all right.

"Do not dare say that out loud!" Alika whispered as he waggled a warning paw at Andie.

The saving grace was that Sam, sitting on the floor and coloring, didn't hear the cat. At least she hoped so.

Andie sat cross-legged next to Sam and admired his artwork. She hoped the Academy would help him grow this talent. Upon inspection, she saw that Sam was drawing, of all things, those three spaceships.

Thanks a bunch, Rhea.

When he seemed to be done with the picture, she decided it was time.

"Honey, you remember when we moved here, I told you about going to a brand-new school?"

His bright-eyed gaze narrowed. Andie understood what that meant to him, even if he couldn't say it. School meant more bullying.

"This school will be much different than your old one. The boys and girls that go there are …" Are what? Special? Magical? Different? "Are a lot like you. Uncle Jason and I went there." She deliberately omitted Brett's name.

He continued to stare at her.

"You only have to go three days a week."

Sam leaned back. His questioning look spooked her. If only he could tell her what he was thinking.

"Honey, you have a magical gift called Draiocht like your Uncle Jason."

He smiled and shuffled through his sketchbook to the picture of the bucket in the air. On the page, he wrote, "He got it down."

Andie could wring her brother's neck for that fiasco.

"Yes, Sam. He can do that. And he can raise things as you can." Among other gifts, like freezing people into statues.

"When he was a little boy, he had trouble making the magic work right. So he went to this school, and they helped him."

Sam gestured to her.

"I can't move things. But I do have a gift." She'd not expected this avenue.

Sam perked up, and a smile crossed his face. Andie had never told him about hers. Why should she? She was a failure at it.

"Mimi and Rhea have the same one. Some people call us witches."

Holy Hades. Did this sound as crazy to him as it did to her?

Sam quickly turned to a new page, took a black marker, and drew a witch's hat.

"No, honey. That's a storybook witch. We don't wear those." She rolled her head till her neck cracked. "Let's talk about the new school. Remember we crossed the long bridge over the water the day we came here? The school is on the Tampa side. And it's called Rosemont."

She waited to let this sink in before she continued. "We will move near the school, so we don't have to drive the bridge every day."

Sam shook his head violently as he flipped through his book, found a picture he'd drawn of Brett's dog, and tapped his finger on it. He found another picture of Mimi and tapped it. Then one of Rhea. And Brett. And the water.

"I get it. I love all these things, too." Well, maybe not Brett. "We can come to visit. If we stay here, the drive back and forth every day would mean you get up early and ride in the car a lot."

Sam tossed his markers across the room and crossed his arms over his chest.

"Honey, it's okay to be upset. We'll visit Rosemont in a couple of days, and you'll see. It's a nice place."

And how would she know this for a fact? She hadn't been on campus since she graduated nine years ago.

Andie retrieved the strewn markers and put them back into Sam's box. When she held her hand out to help him stand, he shrugged her away. The poor kid had been through so many changes. And just as he was adjusting, she was about to yank him into another.

It wouldn't be long before she couldn't handle her little Draiocht by herself. Sam needed to be in Rosemont to learn self-control and socialize with kids like him.

Rosemont had worked for Jason and, to some degree, for her. She didn't have a lot of options, and from all appearances, it was none too soon to get him started.

"It's noon already, and I'm starving. How about we get some lunch?"

Sam's pout retreated as he cast a hangdog look toward her.

"I guess that's a no." Only one way to prove it. "Oh, I know. There's some of last night's dinner in Mimi's fridge." This was the big test. Sam hated leftovers.

He gave her another head shake, reached for her hand, and led her to the door.

"Hamburgers it is!" Thank goodness. Though it was delicious last night, she didn't want leftovers, either.

Rosemont was the best solution, but she sure hoped they wouldn't change her little man too much.

BRETT WALKED through the Dockside outdoor eating area, arranging and adjusting chairs and table umbrellas. At the same time, he kept an eye on three unfamiliar men in the parking lot.

These brow-wipers dressed in matching polo shirts weren't from around here, nor did they look like typical tourists. His curiosity won out, and he couldn't stand it any longer.

He walked along the seawall, stopping now and again to throw a broken shell into the Intracoastal water. The older one of the three, clearly the alpha, held his phone to his ear. Brett couldn't catch the conversation.

He pasted on a broad grin and waved as he approached them. "Hey, guys. I hate to interrupt, but have you seen a golden retriever? The damn dog's run off on me again." A justifiable white lie.

With annoyed glares, the three shook their heads.

He crooked a thumb to the Dockside. "I own the restaurant. When I saw you over here, I thought you might have seen him."

"Didn't see any dog." Alpha's sweat-soaked shirt stuck to his chest.

The other two kept quiet. Alpha muttered something unintelligible and waved his associates toward the car. He glared one more time at Brett before climbing into the driver's seat. As they accelerated out of the lot, their tires spun gravel in all directions.

"Have a nice day." Brett waved through a dust cloud. "And don't stop at any red lights on your way back to hell."

Robbi met him halfway in the parking lot. "They were here yesterday and spent about forty-five minutes at the bar." She reached into her jeans pocket. "They left this card. I was going to give it to you later."

Brett glanced toward the road and back at the card.

Xavier Land Development, Miami, Florida.

"Did you hear what they talked about?" he asked as they walked back inside.

"Boss, you know I don't carry tales."

What's this? When did she subscribe to a code of ethics?

At the bar, she poured a pint for Brett. "Okay, tell me everything you remember," he said.

"You know how some customers ignore bartenders like we're not even here?" She cracked a half-smile and ticked her head at an angle. "I was glass to those buttholes. The tall guy was on the phone most of the time."

"And?" Dragging this out of her doused him in frustration.

"You don't have to yell." Robbi looked around and back at Brett. "From what I overheard, they were scoping out the operation."

Brett sipped his beer. "How would you define scoping out?"

"What is this? CSI Baga Shores?"

"Humor me."

"Honestly, they mostly stared at their computer, and the one guy was on the phone a lot. It was some kind of building plan from what little I saw."

Brett jerked upright. "Why didn't you call me?"

"With all the customers we had yesterday, I forgot until I saw them again today."

The empty lot next door had been vacant as long as Brett had lived in Baga Shores. He hadn't heard any gossip about any developers sniffing around.

"I didn't pick up a magical vibe from them, did you?" he asked.

"No. They were Ordinaries."

Brett finished his beer. "Hope they tipped you well."

"They didn't order." She took Brett's empty glass and wiped the bar. "No food. Not even a beer. They sat there drinking water. So not a single stinking tip."

Once he reached the top of the stairs to his apartment, Brett stopped and scratched sleepy Rex's ears. "Pal, would you please remind me never to own a restaurant again in my next life?"

No sense in jumping the gun. Who would buy an empty lot situated on prime land between the Intracoastal and Gulf of Mexico in their right mind?

He glanced at the Xavier Land Development business card again. Yeah, right. Like all they wanted was the lot? Brett suspected these dudes had something else on their minds.

BEFORE ANDIE COULD STOP HIM, Sam had dashed straight to the Dockside Grille corner table where they'd sat before.

After offering her apologies to the hostess, Andie joined him.

"Sam, we wait to be seated in a restaurant. You can't just run to any table you want."

Oblivious, Sam eyed the water. The odds of seeing the same dolphin were slim to nil, but she couldn't tell him. There were other options for burgers in Baga Shores, but she knew Sam had fun here before, and it was convenient.

Were these her only reasons? Although still annoyed at Brett, she secretly hoped to see him again.

The impromptu kiss had seared her memory. It shouldn't have happened, but she hadn't tried very hard to stop it.

She'd been carried away by the rhythm of the drums how the firelight reflected on Brett's chiseled features. The wine buzz. His warm body against hers. His lips devouring hers. Their tongues exploring, dancing.

Dancing like Sabrina at the drum circle and standing at their table. Right now.

"Hey, you two. Good to see you," Sabrina said.

"Uh. Yes. Hello. Sam and I got hungry for bellies and fries."

What had she just said? If mortified had a twin, it would be called Andie.

"Bellies?" Sabrina asked.

Andie glanced between Sam, about to explode in laughter and Sabrina with a befuddled expression.

Where were those dolphins when she needed them?

Andie tried to laugh it off. "Gosh, I don't know where my head's at today." Oh, but she did know. Who could forget Sabrina's seductive belly dance?

"Burgers and fries." And an order of foot in mouth.

"You got it. Chocolate milk again, Sam?"

He nodded.

"I'll have iced tea." No chance of a repeat milk mustache for Andie.

"I'll get your order right in. Brett's around somewhere. I'm sure he'll be glad to see you." Sabrina left for the kitchen.

The poor woman had no clue Brett had hit on Andie. Not only was Brett a two-timer, but he was also a failure as a chaperone. Enough muddling old history. Andie had a lot more to worry about.

It wouldn't be easy for Andie to tell Mimi that she couldn't help run the store. At first, Andie thought it would be a safe way to ease into her new life in Baga Shores and a life of independence.

But it had been Mimi who'd insisted Sam go to Rosemont in the first place. And Mimi had Rhea to help her. If the cat kept an eye on Rhea, and the woman didn't fall and break a hip doing those pirouettes, she might become a decent shop clerk.

Or not.

But Andie had to remember this was about Sam and his future.

Shortly, their orders arrived. The first bite was always a French fry. Delicious and crispy. Not drenched in fat. A light coating of salt. It might sound crazy, but these fries screamed out for mustard.

She retrieved the plastic bottle from the condiment basket, shook it, opened the lid, and squeezed it. Nothing came out. She hated when that happened.

She shook it harder and tried squeezing it again.

And then the mustard came out in one long, noisy, squishy, exploding puddle. Strategically missing the fries and burger, the yellow paste landed on her lap. And on the table. And on her feet that she'd slipped out of her flip-flops.

Andie shut her eyes and prayed a sinkhole would open and she'd be swallowed deep into the earth.

Her son's uproarious laughter brought her back.

"Sam, did you mess with this lid?" she asked.

He slowly shook his head. Then it must be another one of her graceful moves.

Sabrina reappeared with a roll of paper towels and a spray bottle of water. She sat next to Sabrina, and together they dabbed and mopped up the goo.

"I picked a good day to wear white shorts," Andie said.

"When you get home, make a vinegar and baking soda paste and rub it in," Sabrina said.

"Spoken from experience," Andie said.

"If this is the worst thing today, I'll be a happy woman," Sabrina said. "You can't imagine what spring break's like." She handed the spray bottle to Andie. "Keep the spot wet until you get home."

For once, Andie wished she had her mother's ability to fade in and out. "I really am sorry."

"It's nothing, at least on our end. How about I get a box for the rest of your meal?"

"Good idea," Andie said. Sabrina was a real sweetie, and Andie could understand how Brett could fall for her.

"I hear congratulations are in order," Andie said, though she hadn't seen a ring on Sabrina's finger.

"Boy, news travels in this town. But thank you. I just hope I can live up to Brett's expectation."

What the heck did she mean by that cringe-worthy comment?

"I'm sure you will," Andie said.

"He's a tough negotiator, but I feel pretty good about the deal."

Andie slowly pressed her back into the chair. Was she talking about some kind of prenup agreement?

"I'll get the box and be right back," Sabrina said.

Andie glanced over to Sam, who had continued to munch away, leaving only a few crumbs on his plate once he'd settled down.

"Enjoy the show?" Andie asked.

He shrugged and finished off the last of his milk. This would qualify as a full page in his sketchbook.

"Holy hell, Andie. What happened to you?"

Of course, Brett would be the one to bring the darn carryout box. She snatched it from him while she shot Sam a don't-you-dare-start-laughing-again look.

"It was an accident," she said. "And Sabrina was very gracious about it. By the way, I'm thrilled for both of you."

"She was a hard sell. But I sweetened the pot. She's worth way more than what we agreed to, but I let her think she won at thirty-five percent. And I'm going to hold her to a three-year deal."

What in the name of common sense did he mean? He was talking like he'd just negotiated an NFL player contract.

She shrugged to each their own.

Chapter Seventeen

Jason greeted the guard who opened the gate for them and started the slow drive along the quarter-mile road leading to the Rosemont Academy administration building.

The interlaced branches of the hundred-year-old Southern live oak trees stood sentry on either roadside. They created an imposing canopy that blocked the bright midday sun.

Older kids loved scaring the younger ones with tales of how the trees bent to the ground at night to block people from coming in or out. Goosebumps still skittered over her arms at the irrational thought that they might.

Andie would be eternally grateful to Jason for coming with her. She wore a happy face for Sam, though it wasn't easy. She knew Jason wasn't a hundred percent on board with her decision. Still, he provided much-needed emotional and moral support.

Once they parked, neither sibling said a word, leaving Andie to wonder if Jason had the same skin-crawling vibe as she did.

Nothing had changed. Not one paver on the walkway to the front door. Not one rosebush in the headmaster's garden. Not one brick in the five-story main building. It was a place locked in time.

Jason cupped her elbow. "Come on, sis. We can do this."

Inside, she found herself speechless. Students and faculty buzzed up and down the twin staircases, passing her on either side.

Were they talking in the halls? Laughing? Were these kids happy?

"Jason, are you seeing this?"

"Not what I expected, either."

"I don't believe my eyes! Jason and Andarta McCraig? I'd heard you were visiting today."

Andie turned around to stand face-to-face with Will Providence, one of the biggest, worst, no-account wizards Rosemont ever produced. Second to Brett Austin. What was he doing here?

"Will?" Jason asked.

"In the flesh." He knelt to Sam. "And I understand you might be joining us."

Sam shifted his glance between his uncle and mother.

"Sam doesn't speak," Andie said. "But yes, that's the plan. Three days a week."

"Fantastic! Let's check-in at the office, and then we'll take the grand tour."

Maybe the rose garden was the same, but the office was nothing like Andie remembered. The long front counter was gone, as was the ring of hard wooden chairs around the wall.

This room had all the feels of a welcoming concierge.

"Give me a minute." Will disappeared to a back office. When he returned, he had three lanyards with guest name tags.

"It's lunch break. Shall we start the tour in the Starlite?" Will asked.

Jason and Andie exchanged confused looks.

"That's right. It's been a while since you've been here." Will waved at them to follow.

After threading through the foyer, they exited through automatic double doors that opened to a glass-enclosed eating area rivaling any upscale restaurant.

"Whoa," Jason said.

"What happened to the old cafeteria?" Andie asked.

"That monster came out years ago. You can thank your grandfather. The remodeling project was part of his endowment."

Why hadn't Mimi told her this? All she'd mentioned was that Sam's tuition would be waived.

They took a table near a window that overlooked another eating area outdoors, where students and faculty mingled in a manicured garden seating area. After they placed their orders, Will shared that he went to college after graduating from the Academy and majored in marine science. Now he was an instructor in the biologic sciences department.

Andie would never have guessed he'd ever come back to the Academy, let alone live to see twenty-one.

Maybe she could go back to college one day and finish her music degree. That was way down the line of priorities.

"I'm living proof to never give up on yourself," Will said.

Once their food arrived, the adults enjoyed savory Parmesan-encrusted baked chicken. Sam devoured a peanut butter and jelly sandwich like he'd never had anything that good. In between bites, he worked on some sketches.

A young student, about fourteen, came up to the table as they finished. "Doctor Providence, is it all right if I miss class today? We think the female dolphin is about to give birth."

With a pleading look, Sam tugged on Andie's arm.

"Honey, I don't think you could go with them."

"Sure he can if we have your permission. My class will be observing." Will instructed the student to gather everyone and meet in the aquarium.

"Aquarium?" Jason asked.

"Thanks to your grandfather, we have one. It seemed a waste not to build one since the property line butts up to Tampa Bay. Our curriculum now includes expanded programs in arts and entertainment, gaming, STEM, and foreign language. I head up the marine science program."

Had Andie walked through an invisible barrier to another dimension? This could not be the same Rosemont she remembered.

As though they'd heard a silent bell, all the students took their dishes to a conveyor. Were they programmed somehow?

"What's happening?" she asked.

"Lunch is over. They're headed back to their respective learning pods," Will said.

"Pods?" Jason asked.

"We don't call them classrooms anymore. The kids want to go back, by the way."

"On their own?" Jason asked. "As in *voluntarily* go to class—I mean, their pods?"

Will laughed. "Not like in our day when we'd devise any way we could to ditch class."

Andie glanced at Sam, who looked so small in the presence of all these upper-division kids.

"Where are the younger students?" she asked.

"We'll walk through that area to get to the aquarium," Will said.

Once the gloomiest part of the Academy, the old west wing had been transformed. No more dark, ominous hallways. Instead, the passage between the learning pods was bordered by half-walls. The interior was divided into different seating areas. Children worked with a teacher at some stations, alone in others.

"There aren't grade levels here, either," Will said. "In this part of the Academy, learning groups include all ages. Once they master all the levels here and we feel they are socially and emotionally ready, then they move to the older students' group."

Andie stayed back with Will while Jason walked with Sam to inspect a little art studio.

"I have some questions," she said.

"I suspect one of them is about the child's magical gifts," Will said.

"Yes. Sam's a Draio, and it's emerging exponentially. I was hoping that Rosemont would be where maybe he'd be distracted by other things."

"Look, Andie, Rosemont develops the whole child, including their gifts.

"We evaluate each child's level of magic just as we evaluate and explore their other talents and abilities. I observed Sam drawing at lunch. He seems inclined to art. Some love science. For some, it's sports. Every kid is an individual."

Andie ducked her gaze away from Will. This sounded like Mimi's spiel. She was tired of going over this with others and with herself. She knew Sam's gift was developing faster than she could keep up with, but the decision to let him come here was beyond frightening.

"I'm still a wizard, but I don't go around zapping people with a wand or flying around the building. I see my gift as an important part of my heritage," Will said.

Definitely Mimi.

Will continued. "I didn't fully appreciate the awesome role models here until I got older. I could have worked anywhere, but I chose

Rosemont. I want to pay it forward. I believe the only people who know how to work with magical kids *are* magical."

Hypothetically, that sounded wonderful, but Sam was different.

"What kinds of services would you provide for a child like my son?"

"We have professionals on staff who can help him. Many kids here have differing sensory abilities. It kind of comes with the territory, I've discovered. Our goal for each child is to feel confident and empowered to be a part of the larger society."

"And if it doesn't work out?" she asked.

"Give it a semester. Three days per week should work out fine. Once a student is older and progresses to five days a week, there's an option to live here. But it's not a requirement."

She watched Sam, seated at a small table with two other kids about his age, deep into their drawings. One child looked over at Sam's page. Sam wrote something on his paper that caused the child to smile, a friendly and encouraging smile before they all went back to work.

Will's phone buzzed, and he looked at the screen. "The dolphin birth is underway."

The indoor aquarium had risers along the glass so the younger students could get a good view. Since Sam was the only small child in the room, Will's students ensured he had the best spot as they explained what was going on. It didn't seem to bother them that Sam couldn't speak.

Her little boy hadn't clung to her hand or pressed against her since they walked inside the building. She was blown away by how happy he looked. Of course. Dolphins.

When the students started cheering, Andie realized the calf's tail had emerged. Sam had never witnessed any kind of birth before.

"Now, what kind of questions will he have?" Andie asked.

"Natural ones. And you'll answer them just fine," Will said.

"I wish I shared your confidence," she said.

"You could always let Mother talk to him," Jason said with a laugh.

"Wouldn't that be a hot mess? I think this is a conversation for my son and me, thank you."

Which would be more complicated? Explaining the birds and bees to a precocious seven-year-old or telling him this was his new school?

From the awestruck look on her son's face, she was betting on the former.

Chapter Eighteen

A quiet day at the Dockside meant Brett could take the boat out before the afternoon storms. No sooner had he and Rex descended the stairs from his apartment than here came Sabrina waving a mailing envelope.

Someday, he'd build a secret entrance to this place. If his Draiocht was worth a grain of salt, he could disappear, then reappear at his destination.

These freaking staff ambushes were getting old.

"You need to see this," Sabrina called out.

"I'll look at it when I get back," he said as he walked past her.

"I'd look now if I were you." Her no-joke tone fired an alert up his spine.

"All right. Hand it over." Brett sat at a barstool and examined the fat envelope that Sabrina had already opened. He was less than delighted when he read the return address. Xavier Land Development.

He spread the contents of the mailer on the bar. "Give me the Cliffs Notes."

"They plan to build a boutique hotel on the lot next door," she said.

"I figured they were up to something." He shuffled through the array of papers and then held up a land survey. "What's this?"

"They claim there's an issue with the property line." Sabrina traced her finger along the document grid. "The survey shows their property extends halfway into our parking lot."

Not the first time someone had tried to pull this stunt. That lot was an odd-shaped wedge. So far, no one had ever successfully built anything on it. Brett hadn't pursued buying it, though he told himself he should. But what would he do with it besides adding a few parking spots?

"I'll call city hall and get a confirmation that they're wrong." He slid off the stool and tried again to leave.

"You didn't read all of it," Sabrina said as she handed him a letter dated two days before he confronted those jokers in the parking lot.

He scanned it, then slid the paper back to Sabrina.

"They already own it?" The arteries in his neck throbbed so hard he could hear the blood rushing. "Wouldn't somebody have seen a surveyor out there? Where's Robbi? Ask the other staff. Somebody must have seen them!"

He'd been so preoccupied with Andie and Sam and partying with Jason that he could have missed it.

He held his head in his hands a moment, then raised his gaze to Sabrina. "Exactly how much of our lot would be gone?"

Sabrina pursed her lips and looked down. "Slightly under half."

"You know how many cars that means? Twenty-five. If you can't park here, who'd come here except for the few people staying at this *boutique* hotel."

"Read the second page," she said.

He fumbled for the paper, then read it out loud.

"We know that this boundary readjustment could adversely affect your business operation. In light of this, we are prepared to purchase your land and building for the sum of 1.2 million."

Brett inhaled and then exhaled in a loud growl.

That was serious money. But Brett already had more money than he could spend in two lifetimes.

And after all the work he'd put into this place? No chance would he consider selling it.

"The Dockside Grille is not for sale at any price."

ANDIE ACHED TO THE BONE. "Just one more, Sam. Hang in there."

In the past two days, she'd run the child all over town, looking for a place to live. On the upside, she was amazed at Sam's excitement about Rosemont. He'd filled five pages of pictures with one- or two-sentence descriptions. The dolphin birth was amazingly anatomically accurate. But she'd been burned in the past by his delayed questions. This would come back to haunt her. She was sure of it.

Enrolling Sam at Rosemont made Andie more resolved that commuting and trying to run Mimi's store would be too much. Her grandmother was sad they were leaving but at the same time ecstatic for Sam. She'd contacted several friends in Tampa and lined up job interviews for Andie. The pieces were falling into place. Now all she needed was a place to live.

Like Andie had told everyone from the start, she had this under control. With a bit of help.

Today, after traipsing through three apartments and two townhouses, nothing clicked. Too big. Too small. Too far. Too old.

Too expensive.

The last appointment was at 4:30 at Devlon Oaks Townhomes, a short drive from Sam's school. While not located on the Gulf, it was in a lovely gated property with a pool, clubhouse, and gym. It had decent-size rooms, though not as large as Mimi's house. Not much yard, but there was a walled patio with a beautiful view of the wall.

The Devlon property manager had endured Andie's long list of questions with no idea how proud Andie was even to have questions. This was her first time making decisions like this. She was determined not to enter into a bad deal as she'd made by marrying Steven McCraig.

After just one year of college, she'd been swept off her feet by the handsome big man on campus. After dating for three months, they'd eloped with Steven's promise that she'd have all she'd ever want.

Nineteen-year-old Andie, who never knew her father and whose absentee mother was never around, fell for Steven's promises of forever love.

But those promises crumbled long before Sam's Draiocht appeared. When Sam proved to be an embarrassment to the McCraig family, Steven abandoned them.

Just as her father had left Rhea.

"Any other questions, Mrs. McCraig?" The manager's question pierced Andie's thoughts.

"I think we're good," Andie said, confident she could handle the monthly rent once she had a job.

Yet when the manager informed them it could be ready in a week, a strange sadness crept over Andie. From the beginning, staying with Mimi was supposed to be temporary. But over the last two weeks, she'd fallen back in love with her tiny hometown and its fairytale sunsets.

Her heart was torn between staying and moving away. But it would be best for everyone if she made a clean break.

After filling out a dozen forms, Andie charged the first and last months' rent and the security deposit. Before they left, she and Sam stood on the front porch.

"What do you think?" Andie asked.

Sam gave a noncommittal shrug that summed it up for her, too.

She'd put Sam through a long day, so she treated him to the McDonald's a few blocks from their new home. Once again, they feasted on cheeseburgers and fries, but she passed on the mustard.

She wasn't much company as a million details spun through her head. Nor had she paid much attention to the sketches Sam had been working on.

"Whatcha drawing?" she asked.

He turned his sketchbook around and shoved it across the table. The detail in his work was remarkable, down to the townhouse sidewalk and front door. And a yellow dog, like Brett's retriever.

"I know you love Rex, but we can't have big dogs in the new place. Besides, Rex is special, and Brett spent a long time training him."

He pulled the sketchbook back and wrote, "I can do it."

"I just explained, we can't have big pets. How about a hamster?" Those seemed easy to maintain and fit under the ten-pound animal limit, and it would help Sam learn responsibility.

He drew an "X" across the page, and with a vengeance, he sucked the dredges left in his juice box. The obnoxious sound power-drilled through her every nerve fiber. How could that boy make a four-inch straw in a paper carton sound like a Shop-Vac?

She glanced out the window as a streak of lightning split the sky. Thunder followed seconds later.

"We'll talk more when we get back to Mimi's. We need to cross the bay before this storm gets bad."

Sam took his time walking his tray to the trash can. She didn't want to talk about dogs with her mind on the drive ahead. They quickly got in the car and snapped their seat belts.

"All systems go, Captain McCraig?" she asked.

But Sam only stared out his window. They were both exhausted. It would be better not to push him further.

Grabbing that quick meal had morphed into a drawn-out affair, but they could still get home in time to catch the sunset. After another blasted thirty-minute backup on the Goodfellow Causeway, they pulled into Mimi's driveway as the clouds cleared overhead.

They sat in the car for a moment until the rain stopped completely. "Fifteen minutes until the green flash."

Sam tapped her cell phone in its holder.

"You want to call someone?"

He shook his head and pretended he was taking a picture.

"Of the sunset?"

He nodded and got out of the car. She followed him behind the house and down to the beach, where they found Mimi sitting alone on a blanket. Sam snuggled next to her, and Andie sat on Sam's other side.

When only a sliver of the sun was left, she started snapping photos. Excitedly, he waved to her. Had he seen his green flash again?

She scanned back through the pictures she'd just taken. The sunset was gorgeous, but the camera didn't catch a trace of green.

Once the afterglow had subsided, the trio started back to the house. After Sam took off running, Andie felt it was a good time to tell Mimi the news.

"We signed for a townhouse," Andie said flatly.

"You don't sound excited."

Andie turned away to wipe a renegade tear.

"My offer stands for you to live here," Mimi said.

"I know. But the drive would be a killer. Besides, it's time I started my life over, on my own." And on her terms.

Andie's phone buzzed in her purse. She didn't catch it in time, and it went to voice mail.

Once inside, she listened to the message twice. It was from the Devlon Oaks office manager they'd met earlier. One of those "contact us at your earliest convenience" calls. Had Andie missed a signature page in the stack?

It was six-thirty. Would the woman still be in her office? She called anyway.

"Mrs. McCraig? Thank you for calling back. I'm afraid I have some bad news. You seem like a good family and someone we'd love to have here. But you see, there's a little problem."

"What is it?" Andie's breath stilled.

"We routinely run the credit reference and the credit card before the prospective renter leaves. But our computer was down." The woman continued her foot-long preface.

"What is it?" Andie's voice quaked.

"I hate making these calls. It seems your credit card was declined."

"Declined?" This was either a joke or a colossal mistake. Or they keyed in the wrong name.

"If you had been employed, we might take the chance. But upper-level management won't let us."

Bile crept up her throat. "I've paid my balance off every month on time. I don't get it."

"You might want to talk to your credit card company. I really can't get into the specifics. Perhaps if you could bring a certified check?"

Andie didn't have enough money in her account to cover it. And under no

circumstances would she borrow from Mimi. "I guess we'll have to pass."

"If your circumstances change, please come back and see us," the woman said.

Andie mumbled a perfunctory thank-you. For nothing. For absolutely nothing.

Chapter Nineteen

Who said sleep was overrated? Since Sam was born, Andie hadn't had a natural whole night's sleep.

Last night was no exception, especially after the maddening call from the property manager. She'd had a large credit line before she got here. She bought gas twice on the trip to Baga Shores. And nothing else. Andie hoped her attorney could straighten this out and fast.

After tossing most of the night, she gave up. She wasn't ready for coffee but had to get out of her bed. She looked over at Sam sprawled across his bed, soundly sleeping.

She stepped into the hall, stopped, and craned her ear toward what sounded like people talking. TV downstairs? From Rhea's or Jason's rooms?

No. It was coming from Mimi's third-floor apothecary.

She went up the stairs and listened outside the door. Mimi was talking with someone in flawless German. At this ungodly hour, who could be in there with her?

"Andie, come on in," Mimi said.

The camera.

Andie sheepishly entered. Mimi sat at her computer station and waved her over. There were nine individual images on the screen, each showing a person's face.

Mimi pulled up another stool for Andie and then introduced her to the group.

Since Andie only spoke English, it was a minute or two before she realized Mimi was conducting a class. She took a peek at Mimi's notes. Today's lesson was "Spells for Harmony."

She chuckled. Andie had tried out one of those once but switched several vital words. Instead of bringing harmony into her life, she'd created murky, emotional disharmony. Mimi had worked double-time to reverse it.

Her grandmother concluded the online class and signed off.

"You're up early, my dear," Mimi said.

"Speaking of which, isn't it early for a class?"

"Not for my Berlin group."

Andie shook her head. Of course. That explained the German.

"Mimi, just how many classes do you teach?"

"Nine. Three in Germany. One in Brazil. Two in the UK." She stopped and counted on her fingers. "And three around the US. Now, what's the update on your credit card? Do we need an Abundance Spell?"

"Absolutely not!" Andie would solve this the Ordinary way. "My attorney will deal with it."

"And if that doesn't work?"

"Mimi, we will not use magic."

"As you wish. For now. Let's chat about your move, shall we? What about Brett?"

Hello? Brett?

"What's he got to do with anything?" Andie asked.

"At my age, I have the luxury of dropping pretenses and filters. You two are made for each other, even if you don't know it yet. And I feel a duty to move this along. Your relationship will grow more smoothly if you live in this house. We can take turns shuttling Sam to school. And I need you for the shop."

Andie swore her blood pooled at her feet. Even if she had feelings for Brett, he was engaged. Mimi had to know that. What was she up to, anyway?

"Let's get something straight. I've barely been here two weeks. And there is no relationship with Brett."

"Give me strength." Mimi shook her head in frustration. "I've watched the way you two look at each other. All the other little nuances like how your body talks around him."

My body talks?

"Granddaughter, I know both of you better than you know yourselves. It's love, all right. We can make this happen the easy way or the hard way. Your decision."

"*We* can make *what* happen?" Andie asked.

Mimi's self-assured smile was the woman's only response.

There was nothing between her and Brett except that one kiss Sam had witnessed and was a mistake in the first place.

And worrying about her credit card hadn't been the only thing keeping her awake. She missed Brett more than a little. But there was nothing between them.

Andie sat tall. "I'm staying with Plan A. We are moving to Tampa. No shuttling. No relationship. No meddling and no spells. And absolutely no power of three. Got it?"

"Pfft. You're the one who needs to get it. But I will respect your wishes."

Still steaming, Andie spat out: "And if you haven't heard, Brett is already in a relationship."

Mimi threw her shoulders back and squinted at Andie. "Since when?"

"He asked Sabrina from the Dockside to marry him."

Mimi slowly shook her head. "Horsefeathers!"

"So there's no chance of a relationship with him. I would never break up another couple."

"I think you need to check your sources." Mimi flipped through her binder until she found the page she wanted. "Here's my Relationship Spell. Feel free to use it."

"What I could use is a shower, coffee, and a chat with my attorney." Andie hopped off the stool and headed to the door.

"Anytime," Mimi called after her, waving the spell page.

A SHOWER AND COFFEE helped a little. Andie needed something to occupy her mind, so she unloaded the dishwasher and wiped the counters. She was about to drag out the vacuum when Grace came through the front door.

"Save something for me," Grace said in a cheery voice.

"Nervous energy," Andie said.

Grace started a pot of coffee.

"That reminds me," Andie said. "Brett wanted me to tell you he made us coffee the other day."

"A whole pot? Of fresh coffee?"

"Unusual?"

"For Brett, yes. Sit down, and I'll fix your breakfast. How about French toast?"

"I'd never turn that down."

As Grace took things out of the fridge, Andie noticed the carry-out box from the Dockside she'd put in there three days ago and had promptly forgotten about.

Grace opened it and made a sour face. "What's this?"

"Uh. You think it's still good?"

"Yes, if your food tastes include soggy fries and something in a bun resembling roadkill. Are you keeping this for sentimental value or what?"

"Pitch it." Right along with any hope that she and Brett had a future.

Why had Mimi brought this up anyway? Her grandmother could be forthright, but the bit about her being in love with Brett bordered on meddling.

Or was she spot-on?

"So your son liked Rosemont?" Grace asked.

"The place's changed a lot."

"He showed me his pictures. He's quite an artist," Grace said.

"Did you see the dolphin one?"

Grace chuckled. "Very accurate. Your boy will be fine at Rosemont. If you decide to move, I'll be the first to miss you." Grace served the French toast. "Brett will be the second."

Andie kept pouring syrup as she snapped her gaze up and stared at Grace.

"Andie," Grace cautioned.

"Oh!" Andie put the syrup bottle down and looked at the drenched toast. "I don't think any spilled over." Nonetheless, taking no chances, she checked her lap.

She cut her toast into bite-size pieces, a habit she couldn't shake from years of serving Sam. Then she stabbed a chunk with her fork and swirled it in the plate full of syrup. "I suspect his fiancée will keep his mind off Sam and me."

Grace halted in the middle of the kitchen. "His whaaat?"

"Fiancée. Sabrina, remember?"

"News to me," Grace said.

Hadn't he told her yet? Guess Andie had let the cat out. So sorry. Not.

"All I heard was that he asked Sabrina to be his new manager," Grace said.

New manager?

Andie felt like leaping off the earth. She shoved her plate to the side, her appetite suddenly gone, and tried to replay both conversations with Sabrina and Brett where she'd congratulated them.

How did she get this so wrong? Because she was a master of getting things wrong. Potion recipes. Spell incantations.

Marrying her ex.

Misjudging mustard bottle caps.

And apparently, Brett's non-engagement.

"Are you sure?" Andie asked.

"I saw him yesterday. So I'm pretty sure." Grace sat across from Andie and sighed. "I think it's time somebody should tell you about Brett Austin."

Andie lifted her gaze to Grace's. "What do you mean?" she asked warily.

"How much do you know about the night my husband was murdered?" Grace rested her clasped fingers on the counter.

"He was killed in a robbery attempt." Andie hadn't kept up much with Baga news. She'd had little time for anything outside raising Sam.

"I've read the sheriff's report." Grace's fingers squeezed until her knuckles turned white. "Security cameras recorded everything. I couldn't bring myself to view the video."

"You don't have to do this."

"But, I want to. It will help you understand why Brett has difficulty expressing his feelings." She paused as though recollecting memories, then continued.

"After closing for the night, my husband and Brett were in the parking lot. Some guy put a gun in Manny's back and demanded money. But, they never carried cash at night. They both tried to tell him.

"Manny was an ex-Marine and thought he could take the guy down. But when he shoved his elbow in the guy's gut, the gun fired. Not intentionally. But what's the difference?"

Andie cupped her hands over Grace's, hoping the connection would provide comfort. They sat quietly until the ice maker's ill-timed rattle startled them.

Grace continued. "It only took three minutes. They told me Brett tried to chase the thug, but the person disappeared into the dark. Brett came back and held my husband until he ..." Grace choked up before she could say the next word.

Andie carefully chose what she was about to say. "Brett's living with survivor guilt, isn't he?"

"He thinks his Draiocht failed to save Manny. After that night, he shut down."

"I'm sure it happened so fast he couldn't think, let alone react," Andie said.

Though she could relate to how guilt can darken the world, as her own did about a failed marriage, Brett's burden must be ten times worse.

"Has he tried getting help?" Andie asked.

Grace shook her head. "Even though I'm an Ordinary human who has lived around magicals most of my life, I can't imagine what he's going through. So how could an Ordinary counselor help? I know how private you are."

Privacy was a necessary component of a magical's world. Andie had experienced firsthand that most Ordinaries couldn't understand what having a gift was like. Enduring a long line of clueless counselors and physicians and bullying school kids proved that.

Now she started to understand why Mimi thought Brett was the right mentor for Sam. Once again, Mimi was right.

"There's one more thing," Grace said. "The next morning after Manny died, Brett rode off on his motorcycle and disappeared for three days. Everyone was beyond worried until he came back on the day of Manny's funeral. He never offered any explanation of where he was, and nobody asked. He stayed by my side during the service. Without your grandmother and Brett, I don't know what my kids and I would have done," Grace said.

A slow smile crossed Grace's lips. "Since you came back, he's been a changed man." Grace squeezed Andie's hands. "And the sooner you admit your feelings for each other, the better. Love should be forever, but that's not always how it works out. Don't waste a minute of the time you have."

If things were different, Grace might be right. But they weren't. She and Brett were total opposites. Andie, with all her insecurities about starting a new life with a child. And Brett was seemingly content with his solitary life with a motorcycle and a dog.

"Grace, we're just friends."

"What better way to start a relationship?"

Or a worse way to end one.

Chapter Twenty

In the Dockside parking lot, a copper-colored Bentley stood out like a single red rose in a daisy bouquet.

After a reassuring conversation with her attorney, Andie had come to the Dockside to ask Brett for a favor before taking a load of Mimi's inventory to the new store.

She'd parked next to the beautiful car. Maybe she'd catch a glimpse of who the driver was waiting for. But she already had an inkling of who it was.

This was so in keeping with Brett's father, Mike Austin. Waiting allowed her to mull over how she'd present her new idea to Brett. His motorcycle was parked by the back door, so she knew he was there.

She'd been dreading Sam's visit with his dad, but she felt some relief after Steven's and her lawyers had agreed that Steven could not take Sam anywhere. Steven and Sam would meet in an open environment, preferably in public. Even though Steven deserved these severe conditions, it was horrible that her son had to be subject to them.

Andie had vetoed the beach or a park. The last thing she wanted was for Sam to forget his pinkie promise in public.

As if that would matter if he got excited and wanted to show off for his daddy.

But the agreement also included her staying out of Sam's line of sight.

Despite all these carefully crafted terms, this had the earmarks of a giant cluster.

Waiting to see who got in the car also gave her time to calm down after the double-teaming she'd received from Mimi and Grace. They both meant well, but why did everyone assume she and Brett would be a match? Off the top of her head, Andie could count a hundred ways they would be wrong for each other.

And very few reasons why they'd be right for each other.

If she were honest with herself, she'd admit how being around him was a turn-on. His voice thrummed through her when he spoke, as did his hard body while he held her, even if it had been only that one time.

Or how his lips felt on hers *that one time*.

Gack! She had to snap out of this. This was about Sam.

"They didn't buy jack shit." Mike Austin wagged the document he held in one hand as he tossed back the rest of his scotch with the other.

It was too early in the day for hard liquor for Brett, though his father thought otherwise. Brett stuck with coffee.

His call to his father about Xavier Land Development resulted in the man arriving at the Dockside as it opened for lunch. Mike and Brett sat at the bar and went through the company's documents.

His father, a burly man with a thick shock of gray hair, slammed the paperwork down on the bar and flipped through the pages. "This is nothing but a nonbinding intent to bid and meant to scare people into short sales. Don't fall for it. But if you're smart, you'll buy that lot like I've been hounding you about."

"What would I do with it?"

"Son, look at me." Mike waited until Brett met his gaze. "Use your brain. Think of something. Be creative." He waved his glass. "Robbi, another."

Thank goodness a driver was waiting in the parking lot. Brett couldn't imagine his old man behind the wheel of the Bentley.

"You want me to handle this outfit?" Mike asked.

"Oh, no. I want this one," Brett said.

"If you change your mind, I'd love to give them a little Draio love."

Though it was an attractive proposition, Brett preferred to do it his way.

He walked his father outside. As the driver opened the Bentley's rear door, Mike raised his hand to halt him; then, he knocked on the driver's-side window of the car next to his.

"Andarta Tanner, or whatever your married name is, get yourself out here and give me a hug," the big man said.

Andie flashed him a bright smile as she opened her door.

Mike held her hand to help her out. "Goddamn, woman! You look like a million bucks. And take it from me. I know my money."

"Nice to see you, Mr. Austin," she said as Mike wrapped his arms around her.

Though his father was crude, he was right. She did look amazing.

Brett's father cocked his head toward his son. "You two an item?"

"No!" Andie said a little too emphatically for Brett's liking.

"Watch it, Dad," Brett said.

Mike waved off his son's comment. "Well, you should be. This woman's a looker if I ever met one. I need to skedaddle. I'm going straight to the airport to fly out to Denver." His dad rubbed his palms with sardonic glee. "And son, about that proposal, let me know. In some circles, I'm known as the fixer."

Brett shook his dad's hand. "Safe travels."

As the Bentley drove off, Brett turned to Andie. "Sorry about my dad. He can be direct."

"I remember, and I'm flattered. Can we talk somewhere private?"

"My apartment?"

"Sure." Andie followed him upstairs, where Rex greeted them.

"Sam loves that dog," Andie said.

Brett clapped for Rex to move aside. "He's a charmer, for sure."

Inside, Brett sat on the sofa. Andie sat in a rattan chair that made an annoying squeak when she sat down, adding to his embarrassment about how the place looked. Grace kept it spit-polish clean, but the idea of anything but secondhand furniture had never occurred to him until now.

"I don't have many guests," he said.

She flashed a bright smile. Her phone dinged with an incoming email. The smile vanished when she opened it, and she started cursing like a longshoreman. Brett wanted to laugh, but seeing how furious she was, he wisely chose to keep it inside.

She handed the phone to Brett. "Look at this."

A long line of credit purchases was on the screen, primarily from online gambling sites.

"Whose are these?" he asked.

"Steven's. I requested this statement from my card company. I don't know how he got the number, but he did. Dumb me, I didn't set up a credit alert. This was the first credit card I'd ever had in my name. He'd always managed our finances. Or should I say he *controlled* our finances? Pretty naïve on my part. But I'm a quick learner. I had no clue until I tried to sign a lease yesterday, and my credit card was denied."

Brett drew back in surprise. Her ex-husband really was a total lowlife.

He handed the phone back to her. "If you can prove it's him who stole your number, you should be able to file charges against him."

"It's him, all right. I'm sending this to my attorney. And I'm calling the company to dispute all of them. And request they freeze the card."

She walked into the kitchen as she made the call. Once she finished, she came back into the living room.

"How does this affect the visitation schedule?" he asked.

"Until this is straightened out, I'll have to abide by the current order."

"How do you feel about it?"

"After this, I'm not happy at all. For now, it's all I legally can do. This could just be the beginning of Steven's tricks." Andie's breath halted, then escaped in a long sigh.

"One of my friends let me know he lost his job. After this stunt, it sounds like his family has cut off the cash faucet, too. He's hated Baga Shores from the start, so I'm positive he'll claim I'm unfit for bringing his son into this 'den of evil.' If he can get Sam back, he won't have to pay me."

Den of evil? Baga Shores? "He's crazy, Andie. And proving you're unfit will be tough."

She composed herself as she walked over to the window overlooking the Dockside outdoor dining area.

"The first meeting date with Sam has been set." She paused a few moments, then turned to Brett. "Can Sam meet Steven here? I can see them from this window. He wouldn't dare pull anything with people around."

Brett rubbed his temples. Getting involved in a custody battle went beyond his comfort zone. It could go south in a heartbeat.

Then he remembered Sabrina's prediction of danger for Sam. Brett couldn't tolerate anyone threatening to harm that boy. At least if the meeting was here, Sabrina and Robbi could intervene with their Draiocht. He sure the hell had nothing.

He joined Andie at the window. The soft scent of her floral cologne made him want to take her into his arms again, but he resisted.

"Set it up for here," he said.

She turned suddenly, and they were inches apart. Like soft fingers, her gaze caressed his face.

"Thank you," she said in a low whisper.

He had to be careful. He didn't want her to think he was taking advantage of her. Or expecting anything in return for a favor.

He held her face in his hands and ran his thumbs over her pink lips. This was the moment that could change their lives for good. Or for worse.

He slid a hand off her face and ran his fingers through her thick, dark, shiny hair. She didn't buck away in fear that he'd yank it this time.

She placed her hands behind his head and gently pulled him to her. Her lips met his sweetly at first. Then her kisses grew deeper until the line between Andie and Brett vanished.

Losing track of time and place, they moved their dance across the apartment and to the threshold of his bedroom.

Fighting his primal impulses, he stepped back. "Andie, if you're not ready, we stop now."

"I'm ready," she said.

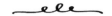

Brett awakened from a twilight dream and reached an arm across the bed toward Andie, but she wasn't there.

He bolted upright. Did he make love to this woman? If it was a dream, why did he have to wake up?

Then he heard her speaking on the phone in the living room. She was here, and this had been real.

While he pulled on his jeans, he could tell the call had ended. She came back, fully clothed, and sat beside him.

"The meeting's set," she said.

"Good!" He swallowed, needing to know how she felt about this afternoon. "Any regrets?"

She squeezed his hand. "None." A broad smile illuminated her beautiful face. "How about you?"

"Not a one."

"I think we should take it slowly, though. Just because this was the best sex I've had in years, and I trust you completely. And, well, everyone on the planet thinks we were destined to be a couple—"

"Everyone but us, it seems." Brett gave her a soft kiss behind her ear.

She hummed in a sexy-ready-for-another-go way. "I'm serious. Please understand. We've been friends forever. I don't want that to end. I need to take this one day at a time."

He'd wait as long as she needed. This woman filled his empty heart and made him whole again. Something he'd never thought would be possible.

"Take all the time you need." He hugged her tight and kissed the top of her head. "I'm not going anywhere."

He started to speak, but she touched her finger to his lips.

"This might be the last quiet moment we have for a while," she said. "When I came here, I didn't intend to hop into bed with you. May I say you are one hell of a lover?"

"Aw, gee," he teased. "You aren't so bad yourself."

"Uh-huh. But I mean it. With Sam in school, me in a new job, if I find one, and living over in Tampa, this," she pointed to herself, then to Brett. "Will be hard. Both of us have stuff to work through."

His gut dropped. "Hold on. I'm not sure where we're headed. But *all* relationships take work."

Before she could say anything else, he placed his finger on her lips as she'd done to him moments before.

Brett waggled his eyebrows and flashed a grin. "And another thing. If you think I'm just your boy toy or an afternoon booty call, you've got another thing coming, sister!"

Horror crossed Andie's face. Then the realization that he was kidding flooded over her, and she burst into laughter so hard that tears flooded her cheeks.

He drew her into his arms and kissed the salty drops away. He loved being close to her. Close enough to get lost in love with her.

Chapter Twenty-One

Sam had been over the moon ever since Andie told him about his father's visit. He'd filled pages with new drawings to show his daddy.

As though the man would care.

Before they got out of the car at the Dockside, she reminded Sam, "This is just a visit, honey. He can't stay."

She held Sam's hand as they entered the outdoor eating area and glanced around for her backup team. Brett was at the bar with Sabrina. Jason, who had extended his vacation, stood near the kitchen.

As soon as he saw his father, Sam wriggled away and ran to the table where Steven sat alone. The same corner table by the water where she and Sam had watched the dolphins play in what seemed years ago.

Steven stood and hugged Sam. "Hey, Sport."

Knees quivering and her stomach roiling, Andie could hardly stand watching them. She gritted her teeth and walked over to the table.

"Well now, Andie. This wasn't so hard, was it?" Steven's sleazy gaze ran up and down her body. "By the way, you're still a fox."

His phony compliments chilled her marrow. She'd vowed not to raise her voice to the man after that horrible one-sided phone conversation Sam had overheard. But the jerk better not push it.

Andie forced a smile. "Sam's been looking forward to this."

Steven offered an empty chair to Andie.

He knew the terms. She couldn't sit with them. And she wouldn't fall into any traps.

"No. This is your time with Sam." *And don't screw it up.* "I'll be back after lunch to take him."

She tipped Sam's chin toward her. "Be good."

When he brushed her hand away, Andie spun around before losing it in front of two dozen diners. In the process, she nearly slammed into Sabrina.

"No worries, ma'am." Sabrina gave Andie a quick wink as she stepped up to serve Steven's table. "Our lunch specials today are chicken tenders and grouper nuggets."

"I'll have the grouper," Steven said. "And Sport here will have chicken tenders."

Andie almost missed the oddly serious look on Sabrina's face and how she gestured to Brett.

She didn't dare look back at Sam for fear she'd break down in tears. Brett motioned to follow him back upstairs. They stepped over Rex, sleeping in the doorway, and went inside the apartment. Immediately, she went to the window as Brett started his computer.

"This might be a better view," he said.

Andie went to his side and looked at a twelve-panel monitor.

"This shows all our security cameras," he said.

Grace's husband's murder had been filmed on one of them.

Brett tapped the screen and enlarged an image of Sam trying to show his father the pictures. But Steven's ear was glued to his phone. She resisted going downstairs and slapping the man into the next county. This charade was never about seeing his son. What was he up to?

Andie didn't regret invading Steven's private space and watching every move he made. After all, it was the least she could do as payback for the grief he'd caused her and Sam.

They watched Sabrina make several stops at their table, bringing their meals, checking on them, and eventually taking their empty plates. Andie never moved her stare off that screen. This "good dad" hoax was about over. Steven had his visit. Time for him to go. She needed to fetch her son.

When Sabrina left the check on the table, Andie took it as her cue to go downstairs.

"Enjoy your lunch, Sam?" Andie faked cheerfulness.

Steven pulled Sam's sketchbook away from him and flipped through several pages. The ones from the zoo. Rosemont. The dolphin being born. The witch hat.

"What's all this?" Steven asked in a gruff voice.

She looked around to see if other diners had overheard him.

"Those are Sam's pictures. He writes stories about them."

"Really?" Steven shoved the picture of the floating bucket in Andie's face. "It says here he made it go up. And who are these guys laughing at him? Some of your demon friends? What kind of mother are you?"

Andie's jaws clenched as she shot Steven a daggered stare. "Everyone can hear you." Including Sam.

Steven threw the book and markers on the floor. "You know how I feel about this magic."

Sabrina returned to the table, knelt beside Andie, and helped gather the items. "Hang in there," Sabrina whispered.

While Steven settled the bill, Andie retrieved Sam's backpack and put his belongings inside.

When she hung it on the back of his chair, Sam writhed away and shook his head violently. Thanks to Steven, her little boy was on emotional overload. Sam stood up and raised his hand, and the backpack rose into the air.

"No!" she yelled as Sam was about to drop it over the rail and into the water.

Startled, Sam recoiled. Steven grabbed the backpack out of the air and put it back in front of Sam. "How about showing me that again?"

Andie didn't give a flip if every eye in the restaurant was on her. "Sam, please. Not now," she pleaded.

She reached for the backpack, but Steven clamped down on it. He seared his stare at Andie and lifted his hand.

"Sport, do that again."

Sam smiled and then raised his hand. The backpack rose a foot off the table.

Steven stood, grabbed the pack, then took the boy's hand. "I should have known you'd muck this up. This town is no place for my son. He's coming back with me."

"Don't bet on that."

Andie turned to the welcome voice behind her. Brett.

"Who the hell are you?" Steven asked.

"A friend of the family," Brett said.

"I'll just bet you are," Steven said, leering at Andie.

Andie reached out for Sam, but Steven yanked the boy tight against his body.

"What are you doing?" she screamed.

"Watch and see." Steven veered away from them.

Brett blocked their path. "The lady said no."

Andie's heart jumped into her throat. She was as much terrified as mortified. Everyone in the restaurant stared. Several were taking phone videos.

From the corner of her eye, she saw Brett motion to Sabrina and Robbi standing back-to-back in the middle of the dining area. They swept their arms in an arc as blue-white light emitted from their palms and showered the humans.

Before the light reached Steven, he lifted Sam higher, holding him to his chest like a shield, and ran to his car. Sabrina and Robbi abruptly halted their sweep to avoid Sam.

Brett held Andie back. "Let me go," she yelled. "What's the matter with you? He's got Sam."

"I'll take care of this," he said.

She wiggled from Brett's grip and chased after Steven. "Somebody stop him!"

As Steven's car sped away, Andie fell to her knees, sobbing. "Sam. My God. My son. Someone help me. Please help me."

Sabrina knelt and put her arms around Andie to help her up. "Brett will get your boy back. I promise. Come inside with me."

Andie leaned on Sabrina as they walked back to the restaurant. Only then did she realize that everyone had been frozen in place.

Andie slumped onto a barstool. "The only thing that saved that bastard was using our son for protection."

And the only person who could save Sam now was Brett. It had to be.

Steven hadn't driven two blocks before someone yelled, "Pull over!"

He whipped his gaze between the rearview mirror and the back seat, then to Sam seated beside him.

"Who's there?" he shouted.

Sitting directly behind Steven, Brett took a human shape.

Next to Brett was Jason, who appeared milliseconds later, "He said to pull over. Now," Jason said.

Steven drove into the back lot of the Rite-Buy store and jammed the gear into park.

"Turn it off and get out," Brett commanded

Steven complied and scrambled from the car. He backed away, his hands raised in surrender as Brett got out and walked toward him.

"How'd you get in this car?" Steven asked.

Brett ignored him and looked over to Jason, who had opened the front passenger door and attended Sam.

"Is he okay?" Brett asked.

"I think so," Jason said.

"Take him behind the car and out of sight. Then call Andie." Brett turned toward Steven. "This won't take long."

Satisfied Sam was safe, Brett continued. "You know how easy it would be for me to annihilate you after that performance?"

Brett's heart was banging against his chest.

Between anger and the after-effects of his shift, he wasn't sure he could control the urge to blast this imbecile into tomorrow. But he also wasn't sure if Sam could see them. Otherwise, the guy would be crisped by now.

"Man. Hold on there. I have my rights," Steven said. "You don't understand."

Steven's trapped-animal expression and mealy-mouthed comment torqued off Brett even more.

"Understand my ass," Brett snarled.

Steven spewed more drivel but shut up when Brett raised a hand toward him.

"You have one last chance to make this right. If not for Sam, you wouldn't get that. We're going back to the restaurant. You will calmly return Sam to his mother without making a scene. You will apologize." Brett lowered his voice to a growl. "And then you will walk out of their life. Send Sam cards at Christmas or his birthday, if you can manage to remember. But no further contact. Do you understand?"

"What about the support payments I have to pay?"

This jerk was not making it easy. "You figure it out, idiot."

Steven dropped his arms to his side and flashed a ballsy smirk. "What if I refuse?"

Brett shook his head in disgust. He looked around the parking lot and then spied an industrial trash bin. Could he still do this?

He raised his palms and concentrated until sweat beads formed on his forehead. Suddenly a purplish white-hot beam emanated from his palms. When the soundless explosion at the target subsided, the bin was gone.

Brett grimaced as he rubbed his hands. He'd forgotten how that stung. But at least he hadn't forgotten how to do it.

Maybe a little less would have accomplished the same effect.

Nah. Go big or go home.

This guy needed to be taught a lesson.

"Any more questions?" Brett asked the quivering, poor excuse for a man.

Once Sam saw his mother back at the Dockside, he raced to her and jumped into her arms. Assured he was all right, Andie eased him to the ground so Jason and Sabrina could take him inside.

With Brett beside her, Andie struck a defiant cross-armed stance in front of Steven.

"Never again." Andie paused only long enough to tame her rage. "You will never see the boy again. And you will leave us alone. No more threats. Nothing. Do you understand?"

Steven fired a slant-eyed stare at Brett. "Is this where I'm supposed to say I'm sorry?"

His empty apology was nauseating.

"If you know what's good for you, you'll get your ass in the car and go." Andie took a deep breath and let it out slowly. "Do not, I repeat, do not ever make contact with us again. And you can keep your money. I wouldn't take it if it were gold brick."

Steven turned tail, got in his car, and was gone without another word.

"I think he got the idea, don't you?" she said, her heart still racing.

Brett hugged her tightly to his side. "Oh, I think he did."

They walked back through a restaurant full of mannequin-posed customers. "What's going to happen with them?"

"Robbi or Sabrina will fix that. And there won't be any darn cell phone videos to share, either. Why do people think they have to film everything?"

Chapter Twenty-Two

"You're trembling," Brett said. "Or am I?"

"We both are. Steven had taken Sam so fast that I couldn't do anything to stop him. Sabrina told me you would bring him back. Until Sam got out of the car, I couldn't be sure."

She relaxed into Brett's arm around her. "I don't care what you had to do to get my boy back."

Brett circled his palm around the small of her back. "Let's say I doubt Steven McCraig will ever step out of line again."

He turned toward car doors slamming behind them in a parking spot near the empty lot. Fine time for the *Xavier* boys to come back.

"Andie, go on inside with Sam. I have to finish some business."

The same three dudes as before walked toward him. Brett decided to take this meeting to them.

"Austin, good to see you again." The Alpha, with a shady smile, extended his hand to Brett.

Brett ignored the handshake offer. "Don't waste your time."

The Alpha's face hardened. "I'm afraid you don't understand. Our survey—"

Brett wasn't in the mood to play. "That survey is bogus. Your contract is bogus."

Gone were any ideas Brett might have even remotely entertained about selling the Dockside. Now that he could see a bright new future for himself, Andie, and Sam, keeping the restaurant was even more critical. He wanted to share his good life with them, the magicals and Ordinaries who dined here, and his Draio allies Robbi and Sabrina.

Selling the Dockside would dishonor Manny Henderson's hard work to get Brett on track.

Brett stood tall. "Take your contract and shove it."

The other two goons retreated inside their car while Alpha stood his ground.

"I'm not sure you're in a position to refuse," Alpha said.

Brett had to admit Alpha had balls. But this banter needed to stop now. Brett carefully considered his next move. One or two demonstrations should do the trick. What would be first?

"Well, if that's the case, how about I help you clear the lot. Umm. Let's see." He rubbed his chin as though in deep deliberation. "How about those sea grapes over there?"

Brett raised one palm toward a stand of bushes. He hoped he still had enough steam in his engine to blast them—one way to find out.

At first, nothing. It had been years since he'd released the magic, let alone twice in a day. Did demolishing the trashcan take it all out of him?

It might help if he held up both hands.

"What's this?" Alpha chuckled. "Some kind of Macarena dance?"

That's all it took for Brett to fire up the Draiocht. He couldn't wait to see the Alpha's reaction.

Brett pressed his hands forward, straining until the purple light spiraled from his palms, spinning faster and expanding wider, crossing the lot and blasting the target.

It was goodbye sea grapes in a quick, white plume of smoke.

Alpha stood like a fence post. Either he was scared spitless, or he was braver than he looked.

Brett glanced around for something else to sacrifice. "How about those saw palmettos? You wouldn't want those obstructing your project, would you?"

He sent another energy blast across the lot. Target destroyed.

He shifted his aim. "And I think that patch of weeds needs to go."

"No. Don't." Alpha backed away, waving his hands toward Brett. He stumbled backward and slammed into the side of his car.

"We are no longer interested." Tripping over his feet as he scrambled into the driver's seat, Alpha sped out of the lot.

"I'll be damned. I guess I do still have it." Brett laughed out loud as he looked at his hands. No way would he clear their memories. He'd let them go home and explain how they lost the deal because of disappearing sea grapes.

As he returned through the outdoor eating area, he watched Robbi casually pass each table, discreetly waving her hands. The diners returned to their animated selves, eating, drinking, laughing. As though nothing had happened.

"Don't forget their phones," he whispered to her.

"Way ahead of you," Robbi said. "They were all Ordinaries. No magicals."

"Thank goodness. That could have made things complicated," Brett said.

"And nice work out there," Robbi added.

He accepted her compliment with a silent nod. Though it felt like a weight had lifted from his shoulders, Brett needed more time to think through today.

Was this a fluke? Would he fail the next time? Would there ever be a next time?

Who would be there to help Sam sort through all the emotions, doubts, and questions that come with the gift?

The stark reality was that Sam did need a mentor.

Mimi had said from the beginning that he was the one. She was right, again.

Jason, Sabrina, and Andie stood gesturing and talking in agitated voices at the indoor dining area entrance.

Brett picked up on Sam's name. "What's wrong?"

"He's here somewhere. He has to be." Andie's eyes darted around the room, and her frantic look nearly broke Brett.

"I left him for two minutes to get him a snack from the kitchen." Sabrina gestured to a glass of milk and a plate of cookies on the bar. "When I got back, he was gone."

"Did you check the bathroom?" Brett asked.

"Not in there," Jason said.

"Or the kitchen," Sabrina said.

"Not outside. I just made the circle," Robbi said.

A couple walked in the front entrance. "Couldn't help but overhear. You looking for a little boy?" the woman asked.

"Yes. Dark hair." Andie held her hand to her waist. "About this high."

"That sounds like him." The woman looked at her companion, then back at Andie. "He had a dog with him. And the strangest thing."

"Strange?" Andie asked.

"Yeah. Maybe coincidence, but we could have sworn the traffic stopped on either side when the boy raised his hands. He and the dog crossed the street like they owned the world."

"Oh, no!" Andie dashed out the door calling Sam's name. But the traffic was so loud, no one could hear her.

Brett caught up with her. "Andie. Find him with your magic."

Chapter Twenty-Three

"It won't work." Andie knew she'd foul it up.

"You can do this," Brett said. "Focus on his face. You can find him."

Not enough time to summon the power of three. Besides, Andie hadn't agreed to use it. The sun would go down soon. Sam couldn't be alone in the dark.

If he crossed the street, where did he go?

She grasped the locket around her neck and tightened her hold on the amethyst. She shut her eyes as the stone began to radiate heat. Hotter. Then hotter still. But she was still able to hold it.

Brett stood behind her and wrapped his arms around her waist. "If I can, you can. Open your mind. Let the energy flow. Use your gift."

Her gift. Her gift. Her damn gift.

Think. Focus. Words.

Andie needed words. The right ones. Words Mimi would use.

Then she remembered what her grandmother had said.

Get out of your own way. Allow the gift to flow.

She blurted out the first thing that came to mind.

"Where is my kid?"

To her amazement, subtle heat tickled the bottom of her feet, spiked up her body to her chest, then exploded into a bright light in her mind.

She knew Brett's arms were around her, but she couldn't feel them.

Then the stone vibrated in her hand. In an instant, she was immersed in bright colors. Oranges. Reds. Yellows.

She reached toward them, but they drew away from her.

Suddenly, a burst of green.

And Andie knew. "He's on the beach waiting for sunset. Come on!"

They raced across the four-lane highway after Brett held up his hands to stop traffic.

Breath heaving, she shielded the sun from her eyes and scanned the sandy beach. A few people were sitting and standing, facing the water.

"There!" Brett called. "He's with Rex!"

Sure enough, there they were. Andie tilted her head to the sky. "Thank you," she whispered to the heavens.

When they were a few yards behind him, Andie squeezed Brett's arm and slowed to a walk. After what he'd been through today, her little boy had sought solace in his happy place. She didn't want to scare him.

Brett stayed behind long enough to phone the others. Andie sat down behind Sam, and her legs stretched out on either side of his. She wrapped her arms around him and buried her nose in his hair. Balancing anger with relief was so hard.

Brett returned and sat next to Andie.

"You okay, honey?" Andie whispered in Sam's ear.

He nodded but kept his eyes on the horizon.

She could still ask one of the Draios to clear his memory of what had happened but decided against it. Sam needed to understand why his father had tried to take him away.

But that conversation, and a discussion about his little foray across a busy highway, undoubtedly using his magic to stop traffic, could wait.

There were other things to sort through. How to get Sam to school. Where they'd live, now that she'd released Steven from his obligation to pay support, she had no revenue coming in. She still owed attorney fees.

And most important, what to do about falling in love with Brett Austin.

Right now, all Andie wanted was a few quiet moments to hug her boy and enjoy the amazing man sitting beside her.

"Thank you, Brett. I know this was hard for you," she said.

"I'd do it all over again for you two." He kissed the top of her head. "Remember what I told you the day we went to the Key? About how after the big blows, sometimes what's left—"

"Is better. Yes, I do. And this certainly is better."

"Okay. It's almost time. We have to be quick," Brett said. "When the sun's almost gone, blink hard. This time, Sam, I want you to count three with your fingers. I'll call them out. Everybody ready?"

"Absolutely." Andie shut her eyes.

Brett counted. At number three, Brett yelled, "Look now!"

Andie's breath caught as she opened her eyes. "Oh my God! I saw it." She hugged Sam tightly. "I did. Honey, I really did."

Brett tipped her face to his and wiped a stray tear rolling down her cheek. Softly he kissed her lips. "Now, do you believe?"

Indeed she did. In the sunset afterglow, snuggled in Brett's warm embrace and with Sam safe, with all her heart, Andie knew what love was supposed to be—truly magical.

EPILOGUE

After six months of navigating permits, contracts, and builder delays, it was opening day for Sam's Place, a children's sensory playground. Brett had purchased the lot next door and, with the help of Sam's drawings, designed an inclusive park for kids of all abilities.

After the Baga Shores mayor gave her welcoming speech, Sam officially cut the ribbon to open his playground. He led a group of children through the front entrance, bordered on either side by a large plexiglass dolphin. The children followed Sam along a path through a butterfly and herb garden.

Colorful splash wheels and mirrors, drums, rotating gears, and prisms were stationed along the path. Thanks to Rhea's idea, a meditation maze could accommodate a wheelchair.

Mimi, Grace, Brett, and Andie stood outside the playground. They leaned on the safety fence separating it from the Dockside parking lot and watched Sam laugh and gesture with the children.

"He's come a long way," Brett said.

"That's my boy." She gently nudged Brett in the ribs. "And as soon as we're married, he'll be your boy, too."

With her faithful carpool team of Brett, Sabrina, and herself, Andie was able to help in Mimi's store while Sam attended school three days a week. Until she and Brett could decide where they'd live, Andie still stayed in Mimi's enormous sandcastle of a house.

She scanned the crowd. "Mimi, where's Mother? I can't believe she'd miss this."

"I don't know. She was supposed to come here straight from the store," Mimi said.

Thank goodness Sabrina was recording all this on her phone. But it wouldn't be quite the same thing as being here.

"Mimi, would you mind taking Sam home? I'm worried. I think I'll drop by the store," Andie said.

"Of course. But I wouldn't worry. Rhea will turn up eventually," Mimi said.

Andie and her mother had begun to mend their strained bond. Not only was Andie more comfortable calling her "mother," she'd even asked Rhea to walk her down the aisle at her and Brett's wedding.

Andie hated to think Rhea had backslid into airy-fairy or was lost in meditation, again. She'd promised to be here for Sam's big day.

"I have to find her," Andie said.

"I'll come with you," Brett said.

The store was a brisk walk a few blocks from the Dockside. When they arrived, Andie unlocked the door and cautiously stepped inside.

"Mother?" she called.

No answer.

"Rhea?" she repeated. Again, no answer.

She and Brett went into the storeroom and looked out back. Not a sign of her or Alika.

"This is strange," Andie said.

"So is this." Brett stood next to a meditation cushion on the floor and held up a cell phone, all glammed and glitzed and unmistakably Rhea's.

Now Andie was seriously worried. Rhea would never leave her phone.

Andie's gaze traveled the mural, stopping at the two totally and utterly out-of-place spaceships.

Wait! Two?

"Brett?" she asked quietly. "Didn't there used to be three spaceships?"

"I don't remember for sure, Andie."

"The one in the middle is gone. Did she paint over it?"

"Got me."

"She's always been obsessed with space travel. She'd give anything to go up on one of those billionaire's flights." Andie's blood chilled. Rhea's meditation skills were powerful. She'd often tell people she had out-of-body experiences, though no one believed her.

"Brett, you don't think..."

"Think what?"

"That maybe she...This is going to sound crazy. She might have transported?"

"Andie. Come on. Even in your family, that's impossible."

"Hello! Look at us and tell me magic is impossible."

"But wouldn't she leave a note?"

Andie huffed a laugh. "Rhea? Leave a note?"

She took another look at the mural. There had been three ships, and Andie knew it. And there was no indication whatsoever of fresh paint.

Andie shook her head. "I have a hunch she's going to miss our wedding."

She held her mother's phone, realizing there was no way to contact her now. But maybe, just maybe...

Alika, I know you can hear me. If you know what's good for you, you better take good care of my mother wherever you are!

I hope you enjoyed BEWITCHING ANDIE!

Reviews are *essential* to an author. Please leave a review on the retailer site where you bought **BEWITCHING ANDIE** and on BookBub, and Goodreads.

CANDACE'S TEAM

The truly magical people!
Chris Kridler, Editor   www.chriskridler.com
Susan Smith, Cover Artist   www.sesmithfl.com
Tammy Payne, Copy Editor   www.Booknooknuts.com
Narelle Todd, Business Coach   www.getmybookoutthere.com
My GMBOT Besties: Cassandra   Electra   Stephanie
Kyndra   Pauline   Natalie   Eliza   Susan   Jill   and Winnie
Debra Grace Staley for early draft edits
Brynda Wolf and Tonya Spitler, beta readers
Chris and Gizzy, who keep me fortified on Gizzy's of Nutley Pizza
Kerry Evelyn, the best all-around cheerleader and super reader who keeps me sane
My husband and "PA" who supports every bit of my author's journey.
And to you, my readers!
THANK YOU!

OTHER BOOKS IN THE SERIES

CHARMING SABRINA Book 2
She's faced with an impossible choice...

Haunted by her dark past, Sabrina de Malnati tightly guards her privacy and her heart. Since she was seventeen, she's survived on street smarts and her magical Draiocht gift. The longest she's stayed anywhere is in Baga Shores, a quaint beach town on Florida's west coast.

Colton James was a rising star in the international civil engineering firm he worked at before an economic downturn caused him to reevaluate his career path. Making a life-changing decision, Colton packs his bags and follows his dreams to the quaint, small, gulf-coast town of Baga Shores, Florida.

Sabrina's return to Baga Shores brings an unexpected surprise when she finds herself charmed by Colton, the nerdy-engineer-turned-brewer. Their friendship soon deepens just as Colton's plans provoke a hidden enemy. If he continues his quest, Sabrina knows it means his inevitable death. The only way to save him is to strike a deal with a nefarious shadow Draio.

Colton doesn't believe in magic, but time is running out, and Sabrina must face an impossible choice: reveal her true nature to Colton and risk losing his heart or hide it and let him die.

Will Colton accept that there is magic in this world before it is too late, and if he does, will he accept Sabrina—magic and all?

Don't miss out on **CHARMING SABRINA**, the second book in the magical, contemporary Baga Shores Romance Series. This series is perfect for fans of feel-good, sweet romance stories, lovable magical characters, and enchanting small towns.

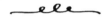

ENCHANTING ROBBI Book 3

Oceans apart in the sea of love...

Fish whisperer and marine biologist Robbi Britton's career rides on her first solo consulting assignment at the Tanner Memorial Aquarium. Her career might be shorter lived than she plans when the guy she almost flattens with her scooter on the way to her restaurant job turns out to be the director of the aquarium.

Will Providence is confident earning this research grant will take the aquarium to the next level, but he has a sinking feeling when he recognizes his visiting expert. Can the aquarium's new, inexperienced consultant reach his level of nerdiness to help him and his students land it?

As they begin working together, Robbi and Will's Draio wizard talents aren't the only magic between them. They discover an attraction they're both reluctant to dive into while they're on the job. But when the aquarium's chatty sea creatures warn Robbi she's in danger, there's more at stake than a science project.

With their lives and love on the line, can Will and Robbi unravel this fish tale and face the future without ending up dead in the water?

ENCHANTING ROBBI is the third magical story in the Baga Shores series. Don't miss out on this captivating, contemporary paranormal romance series set in a small town on Florida's gulf coast.

Read more here:

https://candacecolt.com/the-baga-shores-series-begins-here/

Available at your favorite store!

MORE BOOKS BY CANDACE COLT

A WITCH IN SPACE SERIES

Wondering what happened to Rhea Tanner and her familiar cat, Alika?

You'll find out if you follow Candace Colt online! Rhea's stories are coming soon!

Nocturne Falls Universe

The Falcon Finds His Mate

The Falcon Tames The Psychic

The Psychics Say I Do (in Merry and Bright: A Christmas Anthology)

The Falcon's Full House

The Falcon's Christmas Surprise (in Winter Wonderland: A Christmas Quartet)

The Falcon's Second Chance

Cat's Paw Cove Romance

Familiar Blessings: Book 1 in The Magic Potter Series
Magical Blessings: Book 2 in The Magic Potter Series
Multiple Blessings: Book 3 in The Magic Potter Series

ABOUT THE AUTHOR

Candace's fascination with otherworldly love stories began when she heard her first fairy tale! She still believes witches, wizards, and all sorts of specially gifted characters can coexist harmoniously with everyday people and invites you to join her on this journey. To explore her world of sweet romance with a magical twist, visit CandaceColt.com.

Keep up to date with Candace!

Join Candace's Facebook Group (20+) Candace Colt's Reader Salon | Facebook

Sign up for her Newsletter Candace writes sweet romance with a magical twist (candacecolt.com)

Follow her on Instagram Bookbub Goodreads

Made in the USA
Columbia, SC
02 October 2023